RapAnn's All

by

Laura Strickland

Fairy Tales Retold

RapAnn's All

Cover Art by *Diana Carlile*

The Wild Rose Press, Inc.
PO Box 708
Adams Basin, NY 14410-0708
Visit us at www.thewildrosepress.com

Publishing History
First Fantasy Rose Edition, 2020
Print ISBN 978-1-5092-3172-0
Digital ISBN 978-1-5092-3173-7

Fairy Tales Retold
Published in the United States of America

"Your courage astounds me. I ha' known a wealth o' brave men in my time, including my elder brothers and my father, the king. But their deeds pale in comparison wi' what you ha' endured."

"It is kind in you to say."

"No kindness, mistress, but truth."

"I do not understand the truth. I fear I have never heard much of it."

"The truth is, you are as courageous as you are beautiful." He caught my fingers in his and raised them to his lips. In the same motion, he fell from his place on the windowsill where he'd been perched all the while, to one knee.

"Allow me, Mistress RapAnn, to be your champion and your savior. Grant to me that great privilege."

Oh, the feel of his lips, warm and sure, on my fingers! It made my head go light. But I could not permit this.

"Have you not heard what I've told you?" I cried.

"Aye, I have." He did not release my hand.

"Lady Margaret is powerful. She is wicked. If you take me from here, she will make you pay for it."

"How will she know?"

"She will. She will!"

"It is many a mile to her manor, and you say she comes but seldom. Even if her magic allows her to tell you have escaped, we will be long gone by the time she reaches here. Down the rope and awa'."

"She will find out. She will pursue you to the end of the earth. To the end of your life."

Praise for Laura Strickland and...

CINDER-UGLY: "Laura Strickland takes us beyond the fairy tale and ballroom and gives the readers a story full of pain and heartbreak, wonderfully balanced with hope and love."

~Elissa Blabac, InD'Tale Magazine
~*~

"What follows will make you cry, angry, and appreciative of your own life."

~Lisa O'Connor, Author and Reviewer
~*~

RUM PAUL STILLSKIN: "Laura Strickland has a must read for those who like adult versions [of] classic fairy tales."

~The Philadelphia Free Press
~*~

"A fabulous retelling of the Grimms' fairy tale, Rumpelstiltskin. Laura Strickland breathes new life into this fairy tale, and we see Rum in a whole new light."

~N. N. Light's Book Heaven

Dedication

For all those who cannot see the truth

Other Books by Laura Strickland

Dead Handsome: A Buffalo Steampunk Adventure
Off Kilter: A Buffalo Steampunk Adventure
Sheer Madness: A Buffalo Steampunk Adventure
Steel Kisses: A Buffalo Steampunk Adventure
Last Orders: A Buffalo Steampunk Adventure
Tough Prospect: A Buffalo Steampunk Adventure
Cross Checking: A Buffalo Steampunk Adventure
Devil Black
His Wicked Highland Ways
One Enchanted Scottish Knight
The Berserker's Bride
Honor Bound: A Highland Adventure
The Hiring Fair
The White Gull
Forged by Love (sequel to *The White Gull*)
Words and Dreams (sequel to *Forged by Love*)
Stars in the Morning
Awake on Garland Street
Cinder-Ugly
Rum Paul Stillskin
Mrs. Claus and the Viking Ship
The Tenth Suitor
Christmastime on Donner's Mountain
Devil's Food Ripple with a Cherry on Top
Ask Me
Loyal and True, Hearts of Caledonia, Bk 1
Valiant and Wise, Hearts of Caledonia, Bk 2
Noble and Blessed, Hearts of Caledonia, Bk 3
Daughter of Sherwood, Guardians of Sherwood, Bk 1
Champion of Sherwood, Guardians of Sherwood, Bk 2
Lord of Sherwood, Guardians of Sherwood, Bk 3

Chapter One

What is truth? I sometimes think I never knew. For me, raised at the very heart of magic, it's always been a commodity in short supply, elusive and difficult to recognize. I never learned to tell lie from truth. Instead, illusion taught me that appearances can deceive, and perception is clouded by doubt and intimidation. This, as you will learn when you hear my story, profoundly affected and nearly destroyed my life.

When others tell my tale, they tend to focus upon details that do not matter, such as the length of my hair. It baffles me how such importance might be attached to something so incidental. For one's appearance is an accident of birth, is it not? Beyond one's control and therefore of far less importance than the character within.

But as I've come to realize, such opinions are like magic, formed in the mind and in the heart, as individual as our perspectives.

My story started around the year 1500, in the Scottish borderlands. My father, by name of Jason Redditch, served as gamekeeper on a large estate, and youth had already passed him by when he took a wife.

He must have been amazed, or at least flattered, when my mother agreed to have him. The flower of the village, so she was called, and possessing great beauty. Evidence henceforth argues he did everything he could to please her.

The estate upon which my parents lived and worked was owned by Lady Margaret Beddor. Though she was a widow, Lady Margaret should not be considered elderly or weak. She ruled the estate and the surrounding district with a rod of iron, and with magic, dark and deep as it was potent. One did not cross Lady Margaret, not if one wished to remain whole and sound. At least, one did not unless striving to please a young, fitful wife.

I did not know any of this as a small child, you understand. My earliest years passed in ignorance. Lady Margaret waited to inform me of my origins, till I reached an age when I could comprehend the finer points. She doled the information out like punishment, if I displeased her—which proved a near-fatal thing, indeed, to do.

"Listen to me, girl. Your parents were the lowest of the low, thieves and liars, the sort of people who go back on their word. I do not know why I expected anything more from you."

That voice of hers—sharp enough to flay flesh and twice as cold as any knife—will haunt me till I die. Sometimes even now it invades my dreams and I awake sweating, wondering if her magic can still reach me.

For though she may have appeared the fine lady and could even paste a pleasant expression on her face when she chose, she was first and foremost a witch. Do not let it be forgotten: Margaret Beddor wove dark spells and used them without compunction.

But my parents—I was speaking of my parents, aye. And of truth.

After my father took my young, lovely mother

Belinda to wife, she failed to increase even though they both wanted a child. They lived, as I say, on Lady Margaret's estate, as did so many of her workers, in a tiny cottage hard beside her garden wall, which is how the trouble began.

Lady Margaret's gardens were a wonder, tended by a squad of gardeners and by magic alike. As gamekeeper, my father bore the responsibility of keeping the rabbits and other vermin at bay, and thus had been granted leave to enter that hallowed place. No one dared enter without leave. But from the top window of their cottage, my mother could peer over the garden wall and admire all the splendid things growing inside.

When at last she fell with child—with me—my father indulged her in every way possible. He performed extra work to earn the coin for the delicacies she requested. Yet to hear Lady Margaret tell it, her undisciplined cravings merely grew.

My mother took it into her head to crave what grew in Lady Margaret's garden. This, to be sure, was strictly forbidden—helping oneself to aught from those immaculate beds being a punishable offense. No one would consider asking Lady Margaret for permission. She was not the sort of woman one petitioned for favors.

Some of the things my mother saw growing in such profusion my father could procure for her in the market. But some things grew only upon that magicked ground, such as the rape.

For those of you who do not know, rape is an herb not unlike spinach, with tender leaves and a sweet flavor. My parents' cottage happened to be adjacent to Lady Margaret's herb beds. And, from the window beside which she so often languished, my mother could see a crop of rape, most luxurious.

Green it was, and healthy—thriving like everything else Lady Margaret grew. My mother decided she would sicken and lose her child if she did not have a taste of that herb.

I can only wonder what must have gone through my father's mind. He had worked for Lady Margaret many a year, and knew her well. He must have understood the danger involved in violating any of her rules, must have known that her garden would be guarded by magic and she would be able to tell if he transgressed against her.

But he could not find rape in the local market, or the garden of any villager. And for my mother, nothing but a taste of rape would do.

I did not know my mother, and have only Lady Margaret's account of it, so I can but imagine how Belinda must have pestered my father over the matter, how she might have coaxed and whined.

When he caught her at the forbidden garden gate, he bade her not risk her safety, and pledged to get the desired plant for her.

How he must have loved her!

The first time he stole from Lady Margaret, he took only a few leaves, no doubt hoping that would satisfy my mother's craving. Lady Margaret must have known at once of the transgression. She merely let him get away with it, so he might later hang himself.

My mother—being a low woman and no better than she should be—was not satisfied with her first taste of the herb. She requested more. And more.

Knowing Lady Margaret as I do, I have no doubt

she toyed with my father. She let him think his minor pilfering too small a matter to draw her attention. Then, one starlit night when he once more helped himself to the ingredients for my mother's next salad, she set her guards and dogs on him.

He was brought directly to face her, in the manor house. I imagine the encounter went something like this—

Lady Margaret: Jason Redditch, why have you stolen from me?

My father: My lady, I have not.

Lady Margaret: Do not compound your vile act by lying. What is that in your hand?

My father: These are but a few leaves.

Lady Margaret: Of what?

My father: Of an herb, my lady.

Lady Margaret: An herb, grown where?

My father: In your garden, my lady. But—

Lady Margaret: Why do you then deny you stole from me?

My father: My lady, there was just cause.

Lady Margaret: What possible cause can there be for stealing from the woman who has kept you employed, fed, and housed, all in good faith?

My father: My wife—she is with child, and sickens for a taste of this one herb.

Lady Margaret: Perhaps she would prefer to bear her child out along the roadways, beneath a hedge.

My father: No, my lady. Please, do not turn me off.

Lady Margaret: What am I to do? Allow those I employ to steal from me, will-he, nil-he? My estate would be picked clean in a fortnight.

My father: Please, my lady, if you might show

mercy this one time—

Lady Margaret with a laugh: Mercy? Is that what I owe you?

My father: You owe me nothing, my lady.

Lady Margaret: Correct. While you now owe to me a very great debt.

My father: Great? But—

Lady Margaret: For this crime you have committed, I could take your hand. I could take your life.

My father: For the theft of a few leaves?

Lady Margaret: 'Tis the act, not the object, that looms large.

My father: My lady, what will happen to my wife then?

Lady Margaret: Is that my responsibility?

My father: No, my lady, it is not. But am I not worth more to you with two sound hands? What good is a maimed gamekeeper? Or a dead one?

Lady Margaret would have pretended to muse upon that. Oh, how I know the way she would tap her chin with her finger and make as if to consider, even while her mind, like a gamekeeper's trap, would already have sprung.

Lady Margaret: Perhaps you are right. I should let you repay me, instead.

My father: Aye, my lady. I will work double time to repay you. I can—

Lady Margaret: I will take in payment the most valuable thing you possess.

My father: My lady? Aye, but I do no' have much. The cottage where we live already belongs to ye, as do most the furnishings.

Lady Margaret: Quite right. What is that which you prize most highly?

My father: My good knife, I suppose.

Lady Margaret: I have no use for that. Listen to me, Jason Ridditch. You ask for mercy. I will show you some. I will take the child.

My father: I am sorry, my lady?

Lady Margaret: Your child—I will take it in payment.

My father, in horror: But, my lady, the child is not yet born.

Lady Margaret: When is your wife due?

My father: Within the month, my lady. But—I cannot ask her to give up her firstborn.

Lady Margaret, with a shrug: There will be others, if you do your work. Would you rather ask her to live without a husband? You fool! You should know better than to cross me.

Mercy, she called it. Now I ask you, what is truth, when a high-born lady can speak such a lie?

Chapter Two

Lady Margaret raised me there in the grand manor house, if raising it could be called. I lived with her until matters between us came to a head and my world fell apart around me. And all that while, my parents continued to live in the tiny cottage by her garden wall.

I saw them from time to time, though for many years—until Lady Margaret told me who they were—I did not understand they were my family. Exercising the cruel streak that lay not far beneath her polished surface, she made certain I did come to know, when I was about eight or nine years of age.

"They did not want you, RapAnn." For that is what she called me, a reminder of my parents' crime.

I confess, I did not know how to respond to that. Rarely did I know how to respond to any of Lady Margaret's utterances.

To me, the people living in the tiny cottage beside the garden wall were strangers. They had, indeed, gone on to have more children, a veritable crop of them, mostly lads, from what I could see. I certainly did not consider them any kin of mine.

Lady Margaret always made sure to emphasize that she considered us, who dwelt in the manor house, far superior to anyone living on the estate. "Those people," she might say, with disdain. Or, "My tenants."

Hers was a curious household. She entertained

guests year-round, people of wealth and position, for the most part. Four times a year, she threw grand parties during which feasting and drinking went on for days. While I was quite small, she would send me off out of those gatherings, for things often grew wild. Later, I witnessed and was repelled by the excesses and debauchery.

One curious thing: though I was provided a comfortable room of my own and fine clothing, she forbade me a mirror, and so I had no idea how I looked. I did, however, believe I could read the truth of my appearance in the regard of others, for she used to bring me before her guests at those gatherings, to show me off. People to whom I was introduced tended to lavish me—or rather lavish Lady Margaret, as if she had achieved it—with compliments about what a beauty I was, remarking particularly on my skin, eyes, and especially my hair.

I could at least see my hair without a mirror, for it hung down well over my shoulders, wavy and golden.

One of Lady Margaret's rules—and her rules were many and diverse—stated that my hair should never be cut. The maid who served me, a timid woman, took this stricture so seriously, she refused to so much as cut out a tangle, and would work over one for hours if need be, aggravating both of us.

Other rules dictated that no one should spit—as if I would, being gently raised if not bred—or spill salt. One should never, under any circumstances, be rude to Lady Margaret's guests, despite their profound and inevitable rudeness.

These guests, as I say, had certain things in common, despite coming from diverse realms. All were wealthy. All believed themselves superior to ordinary folk. All loved to feast and drink, often to excess. And most were, indeed, insufferably arrogant.

When Lady Margaret trotted me out to show me off, as one might a hound or a household curiosity, they spoke about me as if I could not hear them.

Och, is this your fine, wee pet?

Is she as empty-headed as she looks?

Common, is she not? Have you managed to scourge that out of her yet?

Lady Margaret would smile her sly smile and make some comment like, "Vulgarity, so I believe, can be eradicated with proper handling."

Ironic, that, since her guests excelled in being vulgar.

She would commission for me grand costumes to be worn on important occasions, even though I might be seen for only a few minutes before being banished back to my room. In the spring I would be clad all in green, the color of new leaves. In summer, gold as bright as sunshine, in autumn russet and orange. For the winter holiday—that she called Yule—she tended to exceed herself. I would wear deep forest green and ermine, with soft skin boots that reached all the way up to my thighs.

Many children, like those who littered this manor and, I suppose, those who populated my true parents' tiny cottage, might well have envied me. Let me tell you, there was no cause for envy despite the plentiful food and the fine clothing.

My existence felt terribly bleak. One should suppose a person could not miss what he or she has never known. Not so—I ached for friendship, as I saw no other children save from a distance. The servants barely dared speak to me. Even my own maid, Elsie, rarely held a conversation with me, and if she did, it mostly concerned Lady Margaret's instructions for my care. No chit-chat, no camaraderie or laughter. Elsie performed the duties she was given in my presence before leaving me as hastily as she might.

What, then, you may ask, did I do to occupy my time? Early on, I had toys with which I managed to amuse myself. Also, Lady Margaret provided me a fine education, which began quite early. Strangers—teachers—taught me to speak, to know my colors, to read and do simple sums.

But that proved the least of it. When I grew older, Lady Margaret also insisted on instruction in diverse skills such as needlework, painting, and music.

I do believe that music saved me. I had a score of teachers—no one was ever left with me for long. Indeed, I can no longer remember all their faces or names. But what they gave me! Och, the music penetrated deep inside me, took up root, and became my refuge.

I learned to play an array of instruments and, I say without vanity, I played them well. The harpsichord came first, while still my fingers were small, followed by the flute, the violin, and anything else that possessed strings. My teachers were always pleased with me, some all too eager to take credit for my ready talents, some truly astounded by my abilities.

Lady Margaret also seemed well pleased to find that I excelled at something. By the time I reached twelve years of age, she began taking advantage by trotting me out both at her grand affairs and for private guests, requiring me to perform like a gypsy's bear and smiling that smile of hers all the while.

When I reached the age of fifteen, an incident occurred that, I do believe, changed everything, and not for the better.

A new music teacher came, the last disappearing without explanation, as they all tended to do. This new one I remember all too well. He was a young man, which was unusual, since most the teachers Lady Margaret engaged possessed both age and experience. And he came to instruct me in the harp.

I fell in love immediately with that instrument, as if it had been made to lie between my hands. It took me a little longer to fall in love with my instructor, but I believe that was inevitable also.

I do not suppose Antony Zach was particularly well-favored. Neither was he ill-favored, though, and he could not have been above a score and five years old. He had brown hair, which he wore in a neat bob, and very earnest blue eyes.

Granted, I'd not been given the opportunity to assess the eyes of many young men. No doubt Lady Margaret considered herself far too wise to employ instructors who might in any way be considered attractive. I can only suppose she could not find in the district another teacher accomplished on the harp.

The manor house's music room lay one floor down from my own chamber. While Antony instructed me, afternoons, the door to the chamber stood open at all times. And our sessions for the most part remained innocent.

But instruction at the harp required him to lay his hands over mine. Beautiful, graceful hands he had, and a respectable talent with the instrument. Admiration for him struck me early and bit deep.

Plus, he broke Lady Margaret's rule by speaking to me, really speaking and not always of the music or other superficial things. Perhaps, being so young, he did not yet know of Lady Margaret's reputation, did not imagine the consequences of crossing her.

I am all too certain he learned.

He would speak to me almost constantly during the lessons.

"You have a very fine touch, for one so new to the instrument, Mistress RapAnn." For such he called me. "And you have a wonderful ear for music."

I soaked up the praise as dry soil soaks up rain.

"Are you Lady Margaret's daughter?" he asked next.

"Nay. Her ward." I dropped my eyes when I replied. I felt certain Lady Margaret and most of her guests secretly—or not so secretly—despised me, partly for coming from common stock. But I could see clear admiration in Antony's regard. Was it possible music could make someone love me?

"She certainly does well by you," he observed. "All these instruments—they are of the very highest quality."

"Lady Margaret tolerates only the finest." Except for me. For some unknown reason, she did tolerate me.

"I have traveled many places with my harp, all around Scotland, and Ireland also, to France and the Highlands of Spain, and given many lessons. Never," he gazed deep into my eyes, "have I seen a student such as you."

"I love music," I confessed, just a bit breathlessly.

"Aye, and it shows."

"Tell me of your travels," I requested, even though I knew I should not encourage such chatter. "Of the places you have seen."

He did, painting them for me in bright colors, speaking of the people he had encountered, both students and fellow musicians, hosts, sages, and fools. I saw so little of people—just Lady Margaret's guests—and I craved experience quite pitifully. I could not hear enough.

I suppose the ending proved inevitable. I became enamored of young Antony, the combination of music and companionship proving all too seductive. Antony, or so he at last declared one gloomy afternoon when gray raindrops ran down the music room windows like tears, fell in love with me. He admitted it just before he kissed me softly on the cheek, an innocent enough mark of affection.

That simple kiss, or so I thought then, changed my world. I rarely experienced human contact, and it warmed me right through, threatened to melt the ice that until that moment encased my heart.

No one had ever loved me. How could I keep from loving Antony in return?

Lady Margaret—no fool, she—seemed to tumble immediately to what had occurred. Perhaps she had our lessons observed through some hidey hole. I would not put it past her. Perhaps she guessed how things stood from my demeanor when she questioned me, for question me she invariably did.

The day following that rainy afternoon when Antony declared his feelings, she called me before her, into her pleasant sitting room, and placed me under cross-examination.

"Tell me, RapAnn, has there been any impropriety between yourself and your music instructor, Master Zach?"

"Impropriety, Lady Margaret?"

She inspected me with her cold gray eyes. Have I mentioned they were gray? Like the sky on a winter's day when the ground is hard with frost. Like a dreary mist. Like death.

Her hair, dark auburn in color, bore streaks of coal black at the temples. She was what is usually called a handsome woman—and sharp as a sewing needle.

She now gave me a glare from those eyes that pricked me clear through.

"Do not play the fool with me, RapAnn."

I began to quiver, knowing I stood on dangerous ground. Somehow, she knew what had passed between myself and Antony.

It angered her.

I did not know what to say—what, that would not cost me Antony's company, which I wished to retain at all cost.

"And," she went on, "do not lie to me." She leaned forward a titch. "Do you know what happens to those who try to lie to me?"

I did lift my eyes to hers then. I knew—people disappeared, if they were fortunate. Or terrible things happened to them. Sometimes quite hideous things.

I whispered, "Aye, my lady."

A small smile curled one corner of her mouth. "Master Zach is a young man." Her tone turned arch. "I suppose you find him attractive."

"Attractive, my lady?" I might, indeed, try to play

Laura Strickland

the fool, but the heat rose to my cheeks and betrayed me.

Her eyes glittered, and she waved a long-fingered hand. "As a young man may well prove attractive to a lass of your age."

"Oh, no, my lady. He is my instructor. I would not dream of regarding him in any other way."

She closed her eyes for an instant. For a single heartbeat, I experienced the balm of relief, but then I felt her probing, pressing into my mind. An ability she had, born of the magic she carried.

"I was mistaken," she said, "in taking on an instructor who is so young. I was mistaken, perhaps, in trusting you."

"No, my lady."

"Still, nature is nature, and for all I have given you, it seems a base and lowly nature will out."

Rueful shame gripped me. I did not wish to be what she implied.

She leaned toward me and lowered her voice. "RapAnn, do you know what a trollop is?"

"I—uh—think so, my lady."

"If you insist, girl, on becoming a trollop, I have much better opportunities to hand."

Heat washed over me again. How could she suggest such a thing? I had been a good lass, always. And I could not help how Antony felt toward me.

I said in a rush, "Naught happened, my lady. We just speak together during the lessons."

"Intimate talk, I surmise."

I did not know what that meant. "Nay, we but converse about ordinary things. I have so few people to whom I may speak."

She grunted. Her eyes, once more open, speared me again. "Has he touched you?"

"My lady, in order to instruct me on the harp, he must place his hands over mine."

"Has he touched you…intimately?"

That word, again. The look in her eyes told me just what she meant. I sagged where I sat. "But on the cheek." Thoroughly demoralized, I confessed it. "A single kiss."

"Go to your room, girl."

"My lady? Am—am I to be punished?"

Her smile became brilliant and dangerous.

"Not at all. But if you are ready for male company, I will arrange it."

I did not see Antony again. He disappeared as completely as—or perhaps more completely than—my other teachers. I never learned if he was but turned away, and so left, or if he never left the manor house and grounds.

I confess, I should have been warned by that incident. Lady Mary Margaret would be neither crossed nor deceived.

And she let me know it.

Chapter Three

As I have said, Lady Margaret entertained often. The manor house seemed always to have people coming and going, most of whom I did not know.

She also had several special guests who remained in residence nearly all the time. Oh, they might go away for a while, off on travels, but they always returned for prolonged stays.

I confess, I had little enough contact with them while small, but only because I had slight contact with anyone. I will also confess, I bore little liking for the two who seemed closest to Lady Margaret, on the occasions when I did encounter them—Lady Russel, and a man called Jeremiah Cole.

I do not know whether Jeremiah Cole was a lord or a commoner—difficult, though, to imagine one such in Lady Margaret's inner circle. When she addressed him within my hearing, she always called him Jeremiah, and referred to him as Master Cole when speaking of him.

He was, perhaps, her own age, of middle years, with a narrow, dissipated face and coal black hair and eyes, which contrasted startlingly with his pale face. He always dressed immaculately, even foppishly, in silks and brocades.

He made my skin crawl. I could not say why. Though he was near constantly in Lady Margaret's company while in residence, I encountered him seldom enough. But when I did, his manner very much put me off.

I did not like the way he looked at me, through narrowed black eyes, a stare far too intense for comfort. I did not like the way he spoke, similar to how an unpleasant cat purrs, or his smile, which seemed far too oily and insincere.

As I grew older, when I'd read a few books and learned of human relationships, I wondered if he and Lady Margaret were lovers.

But if that were so, the scene I am about to recount makes little sense.

It happened not long after Antony was dismissed. I still stung from that loss and had spent my time grieving as well as playing on the harp in an effort to comfort myself.

Indeed, I was doing just that when my maid, Elsie, rushed in and bade me, breathlessly, to come with her.

"Lady Margaret has summoned you. Quickly, Mistress RapAnn. We dare not make her wait."

I set my harp aside and stared. "Now?"

"Aye."

"But, why? 'Tis the middle of the afternoon, and there's no gathering."

"Never mind that. It does no' mean aught. Get up, let me look at you." Elsie wailed. "You are no' dressed!"

I was dressed, of course, in a plainly woven frock such as I wore most days. What Elsie meant was I stood not in costume.

"No time for it," she muttered as if to herself. And then, once more speaking to me, "Let me arrange your hair."

As I have related, my hair garnered much attention. By now, having never been cut, it fell in waves all the way to my knees. This day, I wore it tied back with a single ribband.

Elsie fussed over it hastily before sending me off. "Go, go. She is in her private sitting room."

I went but, I confess, not eagerly. I felt Lady Margaret had treated Antony unfairly, and a strange emotion—quite possibly anger—lodged in my heart. I'd not been taught to own my emotions, but rather to give unthinking obedience, and anyway, when had anything in my life ever been fair?

I descended the stairs on silent, slippered feet and approached the door of the sitting room. It stood half open and I could hear voices from within.

Lady Margaret's, first: "It is my gift to you, Jeremiah. A long time coming, I know. But we possess patience, do we not?"

My feet dragged to a halt upon learning Jeremiah Cole was with her in the room. I heard him reply.

"I can be patient, aye, Margaret, when waiting for something I want."

She laughed, a low, almost musical trill such as I'd never before heard from her.

Cole spoke, as if in protest, "Are you sure she is ready, so young?"

"She has proved herself ready in this, for she has begun wanting things she should not. She is certainly ready for you to begin with her."

Begin? A chill chased its way down my spine. Begin what? What had Master Cole to do with me, or me with him?

"Grooming," Lady Margaret said, before pausing

20

abruptly. "RapAnn, come in."

How did she know I stood there, wavering on my toes? Was it magic? I had made no sound.

Reluctantly, I entered the room.

Lady Margaret sat in her usual place, a high-backed and padded peacock chair of deep blue. As always, she appeared composed and collected, but I sensed…some excitement beneath the surface.

Master Cole lounged upon the sofa, his back bolstered by a wealth of brocaded cushions, one well-clad leg flung out. His black eyes fastened upon me and did not waver.

I curtseyed to both of them, as I'd been taught. "Good afternoon, Lady Margaret, Master Cole."

"RapAnn." Lady Margaret waved a hand. "Show yourself."

"My lady?" Despite all the times I'd been brought before her company, I did not understand.

"Turn around, girl."

I did so, though I certainly could not fathom any reason. What had she meant by what I'd heard her say—a gift? Did she mean me? But she'd spent my whole life telling me I was of little worth.

"Well, Jeremiah," she asked once I'd spun, "what do you think?"

He looked at me then, truly looked, as I'd never been examined by anyone. Oh, Lady Margaret's guests had stared at me when she trotted me out during her grand celebrations. But I'd always felt they admired more my fancy dress than anything else.

This felt entirely different. Master Cole's black gaze picked at me, touched me everywhere in a manner that made me want to squirm. The heat poured over me in a rush and stained my skin.

What did they want with me?

"Stand still, girl," Lady Margaret snapped.

I twisted my hands in my skirt and dropped my eyes.

Master Cole drawled, "Is she untouched?"

"Of course. I would offer you nothing less."

Offer? Horror gripped me by the throat and squeezed. Did Lady Margaret contemplate giving me to this man? No, and no and—

Master Cole gave a rough purr. My eyes rose to his face without my permission.

He looked—but I had no words to describe it. Satisfied, perhaps, and at the same time anticipatory.

"I adore her name. So…appropriate." His lips curved in that oily smile.

"Do not take that personally. Her father stole rape from my garden; that is all."

He feigned a shocked look. "A daring fellow indeed. Good, perhaps there is some mettle in her."

"Do not count on it. She has always been ordinary enough. Have you not, RapAnn?"

I agreed, of course I did, though for the first time in my life, I was to prove her wrong.

****

He left us soon after, did Master Cole, rose and sauntered from the room, leaving us alone.

Lady Margaret waved me to a seat, which seemed odd because I rarely sat in her presence. I chose a small chair across from hers, not wishing to sit where Master Cole had been.

She treated me to a long, disconcerting stare before she said, "RapAnn, you are a fortunate young woman."

Was I? I confess, I did not feel it.

"You have been plucked from the depths of poverty, lifted up, and given much."

If by the depths of poverty, she meant the tiny cottage wherein dwelt the man and woman she'd named as my parents, I could scarcely agree. When I glimpsed them over the garden wall, they seemed well enough and happy, even without me.

I wondered what it would have been like had I grown up there amid that bustle and clatter, if she'd never *uplifted* me.

"You have fine clothes and an education."

I was glad of that—the education, I mean.

Her gaze hardened to gray slate. "It is time you begin paying me back for all I have given you."

"Yes, my lady." I'd not been aware I must ever pay her back. I'd been given no choice in the matter.

And had I not already paid through the loss of Antony? That still stung.

She must have glimpsed some hint of defiance in my eyes, for she observed, "You are angry with me."

"My lady—" I fell silent.

"Speak."

I looked a question.

"You need not fear speaking your mind to me."

That I did not believe. No one spoke his or her mind to this woman, save possibly Master Cole. At least, not without consequences.

Tentatively, I said, "My lady, I do not understand why my instructor, Antony, had to be sent away."

"Do you not?"

I shook my head.

"He looked likely to take advantage."

"Of what, my lady?"

"Of you." The hateful smile curved her lips and her eyes sparkled, possibly with malice. "You had grown attracted to him, had you not? Understandable, I suppose. A handsome young man—I should have known better. Such young men will lead you astray."

She fixed me with a stern eye. "If, RapAnn, you begin to crave male company, it is time to act upon it."

"I do not understand."

"Then I will be plain, shall I? Plain enough for you to understand. If you show me you desire attention from a man, we will arrange for that."

"I do not—"

"Your body is ready, I think. You have begun your menses, so your maid tells me. That means you are ripe."

"I—"

"Master Cole has generously agreed to take you on, despite all your flaws and failings."

I surged to my feet. "Take me on?"

"Sit back down, girl! Did I give you permission to rise? He has most kindly consented to provide you with the male companionship you desire."

God help me, I didn't know what she meant, not then. The prospect of spending any amount of time in the company of a man who made my skin crawl, though, sent a wave of sickness over me.

She gave me a bland smile and waved a graceful hand. "All you need do, RapAnn, is agree. The laws by which I live—those of magic—require your acquiescence. Magic is a balance of will, you see, and one most dangerous to upset."

My thoughts raced, or tried to, trapped as they

seemed. "I must agree to this association?" And then what? I would be given to him like a possession, a—a pet?

She inclined her head. When she spoke, her voice throbbed with a note of power. "You need but speak the word—yes."

I said nothing. Indeed, I feared uttering any word, lest it be wrong. What might she construe as agreement?

I had no desire to belong to Jeremiah Cole, none whatsoever.

"Now, RapAnn," she said, "you have never been a troublesome girl. And as I say, you owe a great debt to me. Think of this as another gift I give you on top of all the others. You hunger for male company. Thus, I grant it to you."

Not him. Not him. I wanted Antony, with his graceful hands and shy smile.

"You understand," she said softly and very smoothly, "I am a powerful woman. I could make things difficult for you, indeed, if I do not receive the answer I expect."

Do not say yes. Do not ever say it to her. An inner voice screamed this at me, very certain.

I shook my head.

A new light appeared in her eyes—one of annoyance. "You agree, girl, that you owe much to me?"

I dared not assent. I sat like stone, though I felt all too weak inside.

Weak, yet determined.

"You agree I have looked after you all your life, supplied your every need?"

Unable to face that look in her eyes, I closed mine. *Endure*, the inner voice whispered.

"You agree I have the power to do as I wish with you—scourge you, cast you off—and none would gainsay me? None would dare."

So she meant to beat me. Whip me, perhaps. That would not be worse than belonging to Jeremiah Cole.

"All you need do, RapAnn," her voice throbbed with power, "is say yes."

I drew a great breath and expelled it in a single word. "No!"

Chapter Four

It was not the last time I delivered that word of refusal to Lady Margaret. Indeed, I repeated it again and again, each time she demanded an answer from me, to the same question.

Will you accept Master Cole as protector?

My refusals lasted for years.

I confess, I did not know what to expect after that first encounter. I believed she would take her anger out on me. No one had to tell me how dangerous it was to cross or defy her. She possessed untapped resources, including those of magic, with which to force my compliance.

Yet on that day, enraged as she appeared, she merely sent me to my room. There, fear at what I'd done in defying her set in. My imagination went to work and dread blossomed in my soul.

She could, indeed, beat me. Even here in my isolation, I'd heard the rumors that flew around the estate; in the past she had beaten—or instructed her men to beat tenants and trespassers both to the death.

Or she could torture me, another activity of which there had been whispers. She could starve me, threaten me, cast me off.

On the face of it, that last possibility did not seem so terrible. But where would I go? You must understand, I had lived under her protection all my life.

Rarely had I set foot outside the house, and never off the grounds. Where would I go, and how keep myself fed? Could I turn to my family, those strangers who were supposed to be my parents? They did not know me and had no real reason to take me in. Lady Margaret might well punish them if they did.

It might seem like freedom, the prospect of escaping her. I had no true idea of what freedom might mean, not then.

None of the things I dreaded happened, not immediately. Instead, for a day and night, Lady Margaret left me alone. Then she came to my door— something that happened so rarely it caused me profound panic. She stood there straight and tall, grave-faced, and asked, "Well, RapAnn? Are you ready to give me your answer?"

I replied, "My lady, I have given it."

She went out without another word. But I heard the door lock from the outside.

I had been shut into my chamber, a prisoner.

Not so different, you might say, from my life up to that point, since I rarely left the place anyway. But it was different; it felt so. I knew I could not leave, and I could feel Lady Margaret's will beating at me through the very walls.

At night, it even seemed as if I caught whispers of her will that circled round the chamber. *Say yes, say yes.*

That, I resolved I would never do. I had not much strength of will but, I believed, enough to maintain my silence.

Lady Margaret left me alone for a week. Not even my maid came near. I had nothing to eat, and precious little to drink after I'd consumed all the water in the ewer, meant for washing. I filled up the chamber pot, and it began to stink.

Then, without warning, Lady Margaret returned. I heard the lock spring before she stepped in, and stood as she had before, straight and tall. Only her nose moved as she wrinkled it at the smell of the place.

"RapAnn, are you ready to give your answer to me?"

I felt sick from hunger, and utterly intimidated. Yet I shook my head.

Rage flooded her eyes. She turned abruptly and left. A servant stepped in—not my own maid, but one I did not know—and placed a covered tray on the table near the fireplace. She next exchanged my brimming chamber pot for an empty one, and left. The lock once more sounded.

I understood, then, what my punishment was to be—isolation—though I confess I never dreamed how lengthy it would prove.

On that day, I rushed to uncover the tray. A meager meal lay there, nothing more than bread, cheese, and a small salad made of what I recognized as rape. Ah, so Lady Margaret played a game with me, a cruel one.

The tray also contained a pitcher of water, and I fell upon that even before the food. None of this would last me long. I would need to parcel it out most carefully, if I wished to survive.

****

By the time Lady Margaret next visited me, some five days later, I felt almost too weak to rise. She walked to the bed and repeated the same question she had asked before.

"RapAnn, are you ready to give your answer to me?"

I summoned the strength to reply, "My answer is no."

Now stop asking, I beseeched in my mind. *Please, stop asking.*

She smiled and left. Another tray and pitcher were brought in, the chamber pot exchanged. But this time when the servant left, she took one of my books from a side table. The lock clicked behind her.

So it went. For weeks—so many I lost count—I was afforded only meager portions of food and water. Forced to ration it very strictly, I grew well acquainted with want. Periodically, Lady Margaret came in and posed her question. Despite my growing despair, my reply remained the same.

Each time a servant brought me food, he or she took away something I valued. 'Twas as if a price must be extracted for the paltry fare I received.

If Lady Margaret wished to impress upon me the fact that I existed solely upon her largess, she could not have done a better job. The time dragged, and I had little to think upon but my fate.

No longer permitted to go to the library, I had only the books already in my chamber, and those swiftly dwindled as Lady Margaret's servants took them away. Outside my windows, the summer passed and autumn came on. The day of Lady Margaret's autumn festival approached. I thought of those times in years past, when I'd been fussed over, costumed and displayed. Would I be freed from my prison this year?

I was not. I could see some of the celebrations, which went on as usual, from my windows. No one came near me all that day long.

Three days after, however, everything changed. A footman unlocked my door and announced, "Lady Margaret bids you prepare yourself to go forth into company."

More astonishingly yet, Elsie next stepped into my chamber. I'd not seen her since first being shut away, and it surprised me how glad it made me, beholding her sour face.

Yet she proved uncommunicative, and scarcely looked me in the eye.

"Elsie, what is happening? Why has Lady Margaret summoned me?"

"I do not know, miss."

Elsie might have no answers, but she took great pains with me, dressing me in one of my prettiest gowns and spending much effort over my hair, which had grown tangled in her absence.

When she finished, and still without meeting my gaze, she rapped on the door. The first servant, who stood there waiting, bade me follow him.

How strange it felt being out of that room! I nearly tripped going down the stairs and had to grasp the banister hard.

The servant led me to Lady Margaret's private parlor. But she was not there. Instead, Jeremiah Cole waited for me.

I balked at the door, when I saw him. I wanted to turn and flee. I confess, I feared the worst—that Lady Margaret had given me to him after all, without my assent. She could manipulate people so deftly—why not manipulate magic also, and bend its rules?

Master Cole lounged on the comfortable sofa and

did not bother to rise when I went in, merely waving a languid hand toward me.

"Ah, my dear. Come in and make yourself at ease."

I did not want to enter that place, not with him there, but had no choice, for the footman planted a hand in my back and shoved. Once more, I heard the familiar sound of a door closing behind me.

Cold terror descended over me in an icy draught. Shut in again, this time with *him*.

Even my lips felt frozen when I asked, "Where is Lady Margaret?"

"Off about her business, important business." His black eyes prodded at me, lecherous as an uninvited touch. "She has left the two of us here, alone."

Unable to find anything to say, I stood unmoving.

"I thought it time, my dear, we grew better acquainted."

Just what did he mean by that? I dreaded to think.

He waved again, this time at the tray set on the table in front of the sofa. A fancy tea service sat there, complete with a wealth of tarts and tiny cakes, more food than I'd seen in months.

"You must be hungry," he suggested in his oily voice.

My gaze flew to his. Did he know how Lady Margaret had been treating me? That she'd imprisoned and half starved me, all in an effort to make me accept him? Of course, he would. They were thick, these two. She would have confided in him.

And so he must fathom how much I detested him—enough to refuse him in spite of her ill treatment. Such knowledge might make a man feel vengeful and impatient. Yet he looked neither, merely confident as a tomcat on the scent.

"I—" My voice failed, allowing me to say naught else. My heart pounded so hard in my chest it made me sick.

He smiled. "My dear, there is no need for you to fear me. You and I started off on a poor footing, I think. But I would have you consider me as a friend, as family, even. An uncle."

He gestured to the chair opposite the sofa where he lounged. As the table with the tea service stood between, making a barrier, I crept forward and sat.

He went on, "RapAnn, I would like for you to consider me a refuge. A safe port in which your little ship might take shelter."

A nice enough sentiment, that one. The trouble was, he did not look safe, sitting there, but dangerous as an adder. Who would trust an adder? Not me.

"I thought, my dear, if we were to grow better acquainted, you might lose your discomfort in my company."

"I see." After one searing glance, I stared at the tea tray rather than at him. I felt ill equipped to handle this situation, or the razor trap of his mind.

"Why do you not pour the tea, RapAnn? Show me your pretty manners."

I wasn't sure I could successfully complete the ritual. My hands shook far too badly. But under his all-too-watchful gaze, I accomplished the task.

"Tell me about yourself," he bade then, setting his cup aside as if it held no interest for him.

"There is not much to tell," I said truthfully.

"What are your interests? Let us see what we have in common."

I could scarcely imagine there might be anything. I took a sip of tea—something I'd craved during my imprisonment—and the taste of it turned my stomach.

"I like to read." Yet I'd lost many of my favorite books because of him, and had taken to hiding the others so the servants might bypass them.

"Ah. I am afraid I do not indulge in that pastime."

"I enjoy music."

"So I am led to understand. Your patron says you are quite talented in that regard."

"My patron?"

"Lady Margaret."

"Oh." Was she my patron? Or my keeper, my warden?

"You are most fortunate," he told me delicately, "a blessed young lady indeed, to have received the opportunities Lady Margaret offers you."

That made me raise my eyes to his face. Fortunate? I did not feel it. But aye, I supposed had I been left in the tiny cottage with my parents, I never would have seen a harp, much less learned how to play one.

But nay. Seeing the trap that lay within Master Cole's black eyes, I did not feel fortunate.

I recalled what I'd heard Lady Margaret say— something about him grooming me. Was that what he attempted here with his false interest and hollow smile?

"Please," I breathed, "may I be excused?"

His expression changed. Some of the thin good humor fled his face, and distaste flooded his eyes.

"Surely, my dear, you would not rather return to your room than sit here visiting with me?"

I would, I would.

I dared not speak those words, but he must have

gleaned the truth. Anger twisted his lips, and he said, "Perhaps your quarters are still too pretty, withal."

I surged to my feet where I stood swaying, pinned like a mole before the fox.

He waved his hand again, not quite so languidly this time. "Then go, curse you."

I fled.

Chapter Five

If Jeremiah Cole thought a cup of tea and an array of cakes would persuade me to accept his company, he was very much mistaken. Yet I should have taken warning from that look I saw in his eyes at our parting.

Things became very much the worse for me following that meeting. Indeed, I more than half expected a visit from Lady Margaret. She did not come to my chamber, but two of her servants did. They entered the room and moved about swiftly, gathering up things for removal. A number of my dresses went, as well as cushions, ribbands, and a whole array of trinkets. I stood in shock, praying they would take no more of my books, or any of my instruments. But when they left, one of them carried a gilded pennywhistle in his hand.

Alone once more, I tried not to weep. But I will admit despair had me by the throat. Losing my books seemed hard enough. Losing my instruments and the ability to make music, the one thing that transported me, went beyond bearing.

I did not realize then that much of what seems unbearable may, in fact, be borne—a truth I was yet to learn.

It returns me to my initial question—what is truth? At times, I thought I'd never know. I'd lived all my life a prisoner of illusion, of pretense and magic. Who was

I, beneath the costuming and the flowing locks of golden hair? Still the peasants' child? Or something more?

Lady Margaret came the next day and stood in the doorway of my room, regarding me. The autumn sunlight flooded through the windows and revealed all the things now missing from the chamber. The place had begun to look bare.

"You are a stubborn girl, RapAnn," she announced. "Do you truly think it wise to play the willful miss?"

I shook my head. I knew defying her was quite likely fatal. I simply could not face the alternative, Jeremiah Cole.

"Were it up to me," she said with a flash of anger, "I would nail your door shut and leave you to perish."

I believed her. And was it not up to her? She possessed all power here—her realm, her rules. I wondered how long it might take me to die of starvation, of thirst.

"Fortunately for you," she went on, "my good friend Master Cole is much more lenient in his thinking, even after you treated him so rudely yesterday. Why, RapAnn, did you spurn his offer of protection?"

"I—" Not knowing what to say, I hesitated. "I do not feel ready for—for an association of that kind."

"Yet you hankered after that foolish music instructor, longed for him. I dare say you still do."

"No." Nearly all thought of Antony had fled my mind, supplanted by misery.

Lady Margaret stepped farther into the room, closer to me. "My good friend Master Cole is ready to take your part. In fact, he chastises me for my treatment of you."

I narrowed my eyes. This I did not believe.

"He fancied you looked too thin yesterday, and fears I am depriving you. Am I depriving you, RapAnn?"

I thought of the meager fare I'd been afforded these past weeks. "No, Lady Margaret."

"He thinks you grow pale and wan. But I told him, were you starving surely you would have fallen upon those cakes on offer in my parlor. Instead, you touched nary a one."

"I did not feel well, my lady."

"Is it so?" She her head and scorched me with a hot glare. "Be that as it may, he insists you be provided good fare. Is that not kind of him?"

"Aye, Lady Margaret."

She leaned toward me, very like a scarecrow in the wind. "Are you not *grateful*?"

"I am," I lied. I feared this. I feared and mistrusted it all.

"Of course, RapAnn, you will have to pay for these meals I provide."

"How, my lady?"

"To repay me, you need only accept Master Cole's company."

"No."

"Then you shall pay another way. Bring me your harp."

I went hot and cold by turns, down to my toes. "No, my lady, please."

She nodded at the instrument, which stood beside the window. "Bring it."

"Anything else!"

"I think it fitting that it be the harp, do you not

agree? For it prompted all this defiance you now offer me."

"Perhaps you could take the rest of my books, or perhaps—"

"Perhaps you could accept Master Cole's protection."

No.

I went to the window where my harp, a small lap model, stood on a table. Cleverly fashioned from pale ash wood, it had been chased all over with gold leaf, a pattern of tiny roses and vines. I loved it for its beauty, but more for its sweet voice.

I had so few things to love.

I took up the instrument and turned to face her. "May I have it back, if—"

"If you accept Master Cole?" She sounded almost arch. "I think not."

She took the instrument into her hands, looked at it for a moment as if examining its quality. Then, with a movement as sudden as it was violent, she smashed it on the stones of the hearth.

I cried out, unable to keep from doing so. Would you not cry out if a friend, one dearly loved, were attacked? Slain. For the fragile instrument shattered into several pieces and lay with its sound box broken, precisely as if killed.

I fell to my knees and reached out in horror. But Lady Margaret kicked at me—kicked as at an errant cur—and shooed me away.

I think I knew then just how wrong I'd been to cross her. She cared nothing for my welfare or my feelings, and would do as she must to force my compliance.

"Get up, foolish wretch."

Before I stumbled to my feet, she summoned a servant from outside the room. "Come and clean up this mess."

Not even a trace was left once the servant finished, not a scrap of wood or speck of gold leaf. Lady Margaret did not look at me again. She oversaw the servant's task and swept from my chamber, bidding me only, "Think carefully, RapAnn."

****

I did—oh, I did. It seemed only my thoughts remained available to me, but even the most agile mind could not escape the trap in which I found myself. I paced the confines of the room and gazed desperately out the window. I looked at a future I did not want to contemplate.

What if I accepted him? But no, I could not—not for any reason. I had little left to me, or so I thought then, besides my right to refuse. That alone could protect me from Lady Margaret's designs. An assent of any kind would prove fatal, and I could not—absolutely could not speak it.

Yet, if I kept refusing, what would become of me? If I remained firm, so would Lady Margaret, and she had all power over me.

I stood alone against her—no safe place to be.

I thought much about escape. There was the door—locked—and the windows. In the stories I'd read, characters often fashioned ropes out of sheets or blankets in order to escape from such windows. I might indeed make such an attempt, but the grounds teemed with guards and other estate workers. I would be seen.

Even if I succeeded at such an escape, where might

I go? Where, in all the world? I had no friends.

Might I turn for refuge to my parents, in the stone cottage hard by the garden wall? Knowing Lady Margaret, would they dare help me? What repercussions might she level against them? These were the same people who had traded me away as a newborn, to buy their own safety. How could they possibly protect me now?

I'd already hidden my favorite books all around the chamber—a futile effort, though I did not know it then. Now, fueled by grief at the loss of the lovely little harp, I set about secreting the rest of my musical instruments. A much more difficult process it did prove, as the instruments took up considerable room, and hiding places were limited. Worse, it meant I could no longer play them.

Another comfort flown.

At least the fare I was provided improved during the following days, both in quality and frequency of supply. No more bread and water. Instead I received two meals a day—breakfast and supper—with wine.

I did not like wine, particularly, and had never partaken of more than a sip at any time. But it became the only beverage supplied to me—no water, no tea. I needs must drink something, but it gave me headaches and fogged my mind.

I began to suspect Lady Margaret had enchanted that wine in yet another effort to sway me, and I left it alone as much as I could. I would perhaps have done better on the bread and water.

Outside my windows, the year died. Leaves blew off the trees and were swept away as before an invisible broom. The gardeners cut back the shrubbery and cleared some of the beds, activities I could watch. The sky lost the brilliant blue of autumn and took on its winter mien, great rafts of gray cloud driving in from the west, bleak as Lady Margaret's eyes.

My chamber had become naught more than a cage. I chafed at my imprisonment, suffered and shivered.

The gray stone house grew chill and dank at this time of year. But I had little fuel for my fire. Lady Margaret might, aye, be constrained to supply me with more abundant food, but her servants failed to provide more than a few sticks of firewood.

At night, I lay beneath all my piled blankets. By day I doubled up on my clothing, yet I never truly felt warm.

On the day of the first snow, Lady Margaret once more came to my room. She stood for a moment surveying the now-bleak chamber before she said, "Good day, RapAnn."

"Lady Margaret." I understood what she intended to teach me through this sustained punishment—unthinking obedience. She wished to crush what she considered my stubbornness. I'd been but an innocent girl when all this began. Now, curiously, I'd acquired a measure of strength. And my stubbornness, as she called it, would not bend.

But oh, I feared the look in her cold eyes as she surveyed the place. What would she take from me this time?

With her sharp smile she said, "Master Cole sends his greetings."

My heart sank. I'd dared to hope Master Cole might lose interest, that some other woman would catch his eye—God help her—and I might then be released from this mad contest of wills.

I said nothing. Lady Margaret fixed me with a hard stare and added, "He bids me ask whether you have changed your mind."

I lifted my chin. "I have not."

"RapAnn, this continued defiance will benefit you little. How do you expect it to end?"

I had been busy contemplating just that question, and liked none of my conclusions. Fear threatened to overwhelm me when I imagined it.

"Perhaps," she feigned a thoughtful tone, "I should have known better. Your parents were thieves. Could you grow into aught but a grasping minx without a grateful bone in her body?"

She would make me feel bad about myself. How much worse might I feel if I accepted Jeremiah Cole's company?

All that protected me were the rules governing her magic, and a steadfast heart.

"I have given you much, RapAnn."

"You have, my lady."

"'Tis within my rights to withdraw what was so freely given."

She called to the servants who inevitably hovered outside the door. "Come, take the blankets from her bed."

No.

"And her warmest gowns. And—" Lady Margaret stood for an instant with her eyes closed, as if sensing the very air. "There are books hidden in that nook beside the fireplace. Take them also."

No, no, no.

She smiled at me. "We dare not leave them, or you

43

may burn them for heat."

When she left me, when the servants followed her out bearing my blankets and my treasured books, I knew the truth.

She would not stop until she took *all*.

Chapter Six

I might have admitted defeat then—aye, perhaps I should have. I wept as I shivered in my bed that night, lying beneath all the clothing I could gather up. But as I say, something had been fostered in me, a strength, and an odd maturity.

I awoke next morning to a fire gone dead and no fuel to kindle another. I rubbed the fog—half frozen—from the inside of the glass, peered out, and wondered how I could survive this. Beyond my windows, the world lay white, and a stiff wind teased the snow into stark ridges.

After breakfast arrived, ferried in by emotionless servants—for I'd not seen Elsie since the day I met with Jeremiah Cole—I took the hangings down from the bed. Not an easy task, and I struggled with it. Yet they'd been sewn from heavy brocade and might be used to give me some warmth.

Then I cleared more frost from the glass, that I might look out—my sole remaining activity. Not much took place directly below. Two workers cleared snow from the paths that threaded the garden. But in the little stone cottage outside the wall, much happened indeed.

I had to scrape away still more fog and press my cheek to the cold glass in order to see them—the occupants of the household had come out to play.

There were five of them, and they seemed to range

in age from slightly younger than me to perhaps three or four years. For the children of thieves, they seemed unaccountably happy. They frolicked in the snow, tossing handfuls of it at one another, and even fashioning balls which they tossed, no doubt accompanied by laughter I could not hear.

But aye, they appeared to be laughing and in grand spirits. When the smaller ones tumbled down, the elders—no doubt sent out to clear the path—picked them up again.

A man came out from the cottage—my father. I thought he would chastise the children for their lack of industry, but instead he joined in the play, swung one of the little ones about, and tossed some balls of snow.

My family. My blood. I might have been there with them, the eldest of that brood. Instead, they had forgotten me.

Would I ever matter to anyone?

But aye, I thought sourly. For did I not matter to Jeremiah Cole?

****

A seductive thought that proved to be in the days to come. How it nibbled at my hard-won determination! I did not understand why Jeremiah Cole wanted me—could scarcely imagine. Lady Margaret called me stupid and fractious. I'd never seen myself in a glass, and despite the comments of Lady Margaret's guests, I did not suppose I might be beautiful. The most I knew of beauty revolved around sumptuous clothing, and I no longer possessed any of that.

If I went to Jeremiah Cole, I might then mean something to someone.

The idea haunted me, along with its sister

thought—perhaps he wasn't so bad. Quite possibly I'd misjudged him. He might be prepared to cherish me. And his company, his affection should I win it, might well be better than the barren wasteland I currently inhabited.

With distance, I see how close I came then to breaking. Lady Margaret had nearly won.

But then that faultless lady pushed me a step too far.

Up until then, her game had been very nearly flawless. She had intimidated, threatened, and deprived me. She had worn away my endurance and made every future I could imagine appear intolerable—all but one.

Now she came to me once again on a cold winter's day, when ice covered the insides of my chamber windows and the wind howled around the stones of the manor house. My fingers had turned blue some days ago, and despair possessed my heart.

I'd been trying to read one of my few remaining books, by what little light penetrated the windows, for she'd stopped supplying me with candles. I looked up when I heard the lock release, and leaped to my feet.

She swept in—I have no other word for it—clad in a velvet gown and a stole made of fur. How I longed to have that stole around my shoulders for but a few moments of true warmth!

But I would ask her for nothing.

That thought thundered through my head even as the door shut behind her, enclosing us alone.

"What a bleak place this is," she observed, looking not at the room but at me, "and cold. I wonder that you can tolerate it, RapAnn."

She crossed to the hearth, which contained nothing

more than cold ash, and extended her hand. She closed her eyes and whispered words I could not hear.

Flame sprang forth on the stones. I knew not upon what they burned, but they made a veritable conflagration.

They drew me the way a lodestone draws iron. I could no more keep away than cut off my own fingers.

"Ah." I did not mean to speak the word.

"I refuse to be cold while I am here. RapAnn, it is enough—I am done with these games." She looked me squarely in the eye. "I have wasted sufficient time with you. The winter solstice fast approaches. I wish our festivities to include your presentation to Master Cole."

Presentation. So she might name it.

I parted my lips to frame the word *no*.

Before I could, she barked, "Do not speak that word, RapAnn. Do not speak at all if that is what you mean to say. This will occur, or there will be dire consequences."

Dire? What had I endured all these months, if not the most dire of living conditions?

She went on as if I'd given my assent. "I am planning a grand celebration. You will be presented to Master Cole beneath the evergreen boughs—my gift!— and you will be clad all in green and white ermine. The seamstresses work, even now, on the gown."

So confident, was she? And why shouldn't she be? There I stood in my thin clothing and worn slippers, owning almost nothing. She offered—what?

As if she heard my thoughts, she went on. "Your belongings, of course, will be restored to you. All your books and your instruments."

"What of my harp?"

She grimaced. "The harp was a bad idea. You will play it no longer."

And what of my anger? My indignation? My reluctance to be gifted like a lapdog?

She had all power over me—or, almost all.

"You need only say yes, RapAnn, to make everything better. Give me the answer now, and do not spoil the festivities."

I searched her eyes. Trickery lay there, and a terrifying intelligence.

"My chamber—it would be restored?"

She waved an impatient hand. "You will move from here. New rooms are being prepared for you and Master Cole, adjacent to one another—convenient for him to visit you whenever he may choose."

She wished to make it sound pleasant, but it did not seem so to my ears.

I shook my head.

"Before you refuse, let me tell you what will happen if you fail to agree. The last of your books will go. And your instruments. I know exactly where you have hidden them. I shall remove the bed, so you may sleep on the floor. The windows will be boarded up and the rest of your clothing taken." She leaned toward me. "You will have nothing."

Except my self-respect.

Despite the warmth of the fire, I shivered where I stood. I could see it all. I did not want to live through it.

"May I see Master Cole? I would like to deliver my answer directly to him."

She thought she had won—I saw the flash of victory in her eyes.

"Certainly." She clapped her hands. When a

servant appeared, she told him, "Bring the maid, Elsie."

And, to me, "You cannot go to him looking the way you do."

****

Elsie wept the whole time she tended me. I did not know why. I'd never supposed she cared enough about me to become upset on my behalf, and could not imagine my fate—good or ill—meant anything to her. But the tears flowed as she dressed me in a gown she brought in with her, and the whole time she worked over my sadly tangled hair, which now reached past my knees.

I said no word to her but trembled where I stood. I knew I must hold hard to my courage—and that I would find no mercy in Lady Margaret.

When at last I stood ready, clad in a warm blue gown and with my hair loose around my shoulders, Lady Margaret returned. She led me from my prison down the stairs, not to her private parlor where I'd been before, but to another room in a wing of the house where I'd never ventured.

I grew dizzy with hope and determination, as I went. I had but one chance—no more—to save myself, and it lay with the man who waited for me.

Chapter Seven

When Lady Margaret ushered me into the chamber, Jeremiah Cole turned from the window where he stood. Outside, snow fell, and the brightness of it made of him a silhouette, all black and silver. A black velvet suit, the sleeves covered in embroidery, and a silver cravat beneath his chin lent an air of lavish elegance.

I could not see the expression in his eyes.

All the way there, I'd hoped Lady Margaret might leave us as she had last time. I possessed so little with which to fight this battle. I could not possibly make my bid beneath her cold gaze.

"Here you are, Jeremiah," she said to him as we stepped in. "It took long enough. But did I not promise?"

He said nothing. Strung tight as a harp string, neither did I.

Lady Margaret grunted and, to my massive relief, stepped out. The door whispered shut behind her.

The room seemed to be a parlor—one private to him, perhaps. I did not know, nor truly care. I took several steps forward and threw myself at Jeremiah Cole's feet.

He drew a breath—shocked? Surprised, certainly.

"My dear!" he cried. "What is this?"

I struggled to identify what I heard in his voice. Surprise, aye, and also a bright note of victory. Like

Lady Margaret, he thought he had won.

"Please," I murmured. I had but this one opportunity to save myself. I did not mean to squander the chance. But in order to seize it, I would have to bend my dignity.

"Get up, child."

For the first time ever, he touched me. His fingers felt like claws on my elbow as he raised me up.

How I shrank from that touch! But I could not let him see it.

"Come," he bade me, not unkindly. "Sit."

A settle stood before a good fire. He led me there, and we both sat.

I wanted to look him in the eye—had meant to do so, as I made my appeal, but when it came to it, I found I could not. Instead, I glanced at his hands, one of which still held mine, at the silver cravat, at his chin.

"My dear," he said, "you have had a trying time. You made things far more difficult for yourself than need be. I am glad you have now come to your senses."

Had I? Or was I about to make the most foolish gambit of my life?

"Please," I said again. I'd rehearsed the words all the while Elsie dressed and groomed me, but now they fled my head, chased by the sensation of his fingers on mine. "I wanted to ask you…"

When my voice died away, he prompted, "What your life will be like once you are mine? 'Twill be ever so pleasant. We shall live here, in this set of rooms your kind patroness has so generously provided."

Kind?

"We shall spend all my spare time together, and you shall not want for aught ever again."

He made it sound so appealing. No mention of all the dark nights sandwiched between those pleasant days.

"I am not sure I understand—"

"You will, my child. All shall be made clear to you, once we are together."

Determinedly, I finished my thought, "—why you want me."

He clicked his tongue, as if chiding my stupidity. "Who would not want such a treasure? Your hair, your face, your form—"

I had never seen myself, not all of myself, anyway. But oh, I felt loathing then for what I must be. For my appearance had brought me to this. It was all he saw when he looked at me.

I bowed my head. "Master Cole, I ask you for mercy."

"Mercy?" He repeated the word as if he'd never before heard it. "Of course I will be as gentle with you as I can be, as my passion will allow. You are young and tender—"

Oh, the emotion in his voice then! It flowed like oil, it gloated with both anticipation and something far darker.

As steadily as possible, I said, "Only you can intervene with Lady Margaret on my behalf. Only you can save me."

"Save you?"

"From—from this madness." I did lift my gaze to his then. Desperation allowed it. His eyes, black and flat as a winter pond, seemed to consume my gaze, and draw it in.

I said all in a rush, the words coming back to me

higgledy-piggledy, "Only you can make her give up on this bid. Please, please tell Lady Margaret you do not want me after all, and so free me from this obligation that sits so heavy upon my spirit. You do not know me. There is no real reason you should wish to have me. Lady Margaret has made this into a battle of wills. But if you tell her you are no longer interested, do you not see? It is my one hope—my one chance of escape."

He blinked at me rapidly. "Escape? You still wish to escape me?"

"And so I do throw myself upon your mercy. For surely, surely you do not want someone who does not want you in return?"

It had made such sense, back in my room. To my understanding, the logic of it was undeniable, but now I saw his eyes grow still colder.

I realized, too late, my appeal did not flatter him. But caught in a fight for my survival, how could I consider that?

"Stupid child." He withdrew his fingers from mine. "You suppose it matters to me that you do not desire me? Of course, I should prefer it. But you know nothing of the pleasures of the flesh. It is one of the things I will teach you, one of the very first things."

My heart sank violently. He must have seen the despair flood my eyes, yet he smiled.

"You come asking mercy from me?"

I nodded, though most of my hope had fled. I could no longer speak, and tears filled my throat.

He leaned toward me, so close his breath skittered across my cheek. "Then nay, child—you do not know me—yet."

****

54

"You have offended my friend!" Lady Margaret shrieked the words at me. "One of my oldest and dearest companions. In doing so, you have offended me."

I stood before her in the center of my room, where I'd returned following the disastrous meeting with Master Cole. It looked so barren, after my glimpse of the parlor, and felt so cold. But Lady Margaret's anger, like a banked fire, threatened to scorch me.

"You tricked me and sought to deceive me, RapAnn. You led me to believe you meant to give Master Cole your agreement, your acceptance. Instead, you insulted him."

Aye, I supposed I had. I'd not looked at it that way—I'd merely reached for the one means I could find to save myself.

No saving, at all.

"I did not intend to insult him."

"Yet you have. You are a stubborn, willful, and very ungrateful lass. You are more trouble than you are worth to me."

"Then cast me off!" I cried in desperation. "Release me from all this. Put me out in the cold. Have nothing more to do with me."

"You would like that, would you not, RapAnn?" She smiled the smile I dreaded to see. "It would mean you had won."

So if she would not cast me off, what did she mean to do? I wondered fearfully. A return to imprisonment here, with my remaining comforts withdrawn?

I told myself I could withstand it. But nay, I did not truly feel certain.

She drew herself up, and I felt the power inside her

like a coiled whip. "RapAnn, I must ask you one more time, will you accept Master Cole?"

Somehow I formed the word with my stiff lips. "No."

She stepped toward me. "Then you have chosen your fate. I shall give you one more chance to change your mind. Then you will reap what you have sown."

She went out, leaving me to the cold room. I thought, aye, I understood the fate I had chosen. For all that night and the three days that followed, I waited for the servants to come, to take the bed and the rest of my clothing and books, as she'd threatened. She would leave me naked here, to freeze and sicken.

It did not happen. Indeed, I did not understand the full extent of her rage, then. I would soon learn.

****

The blow came on a frigid winter's morning not long before the solstice. I could no longer see anything through my windows, for they lay too thickly covered with ice. I could only imagine that Lady Margaret's customary elaborate plans for the festival must be in hand.

I'd just risen from my chilly bed when, without warning, the door of my room swung open. Lady Margaret swept in.

"Come," she told me.

My heart plummeted. Would she defy her own rules and give me to Jeremiah Cole after all? Nay, for her magical laws fairly guided her life.

I looked at the men who accompanied her, both members of her guard, and managed a single word. "Where—"

"You, RapAnn, have chosen your fate, along with

your prison."

Prison? Was this one not terrible enough? Did she intend to shut me into some stone cell?

Suddenly my chamber, barren as it might be, seemed a haven.

We went out from my room, along the corridor, and down the stairs. Jeremiah Cole stood outside the door of the grand parlor. Lady Margaret paused beside him.

"RapAnn, I promised you one last chance to change your mind."

I looked away from Master Cole's eyes, and the avid look that lay there. I shook my head.

Lady Margaret grunted and swept me on with a gesture. Out the great front doors we went, into the stinging cold—I without so much as a shawl—where a carriage stood waiting. Only then did I grasp that, though I had no cloak, Lady Margaret stood ready for traveling.

Did she mean to follow my request after all? Take me out to the countryside and cast me off?

The guards ushered us inside the vehicle, took up their stations on front and back of the coach, and we moved off with a jerk that turned my stomach. Terror closed my throat, and my voice croaked when I asked, "Where are we bound?"

"Be silent."

We soon left the manor house and its accompanying village behind, and the countryside beyond the window of the coach became very wild, indeed. Windswept snow and heavy frost cloaked the hills, and gray skies met my gaze.

I did not suppose I could survive long in such an

environment. Already, the interior of the coach had me quaking with the cold. Lady Margaret had her fur wrap, a lap rug, and a tiny brazier for her feet. Curled up on the seat opposite her, I had only my arms to wrap around me.

I'd been allowed to bring nothing on this journey—none of my few, secreted treasures—and I ached with loss.

For hours we traveled, and she did not speak to me. Her profile, against the opposite window, looked stiff as iron. Her will and her anger had become one.

The coach climbed for some distance into the hills before entering a forest. The forest, at length, became so dense with trees the coach could no longer make headway, and we halted.

"Come," Lady Margaret ordered. "We walk from here."

Walk? I had no cloak and only tattered slippers for my feet. Aye, surely she meant to abandon me here, and leave me to die—and perhaps just as well. Let the pain end.

But my pain had just begun.

We did not walk far. No path existed, although Lady Margaret, in the lead, found a way. I understood now she must follow some magical compass. I trailed her, and the guards came after, with their daggers drawn.

We came at last to a clearing. By now, at late afternoon, the light began to fade. Stark shadows etched the structure that stood there.

A tower. Built of stone it was, high and narrow, with a turret roof. I saw no door and only a single window, set very high up, nearly beneath the edge of that roof. It looked stark and new, and bore a visible haze of magic.

Stone on stone, I thought. It had been laid by magic, stone on stone.

God help me, I did not understand, not till Lady Margaret paused and said in a voice like ice, "Your new prison."

Here? Me? No, oh, no—

I wanted to run. The impulse passed very clearly through my mind. But where? We'd traveled through miles of empty country and forest.

To flee was to perish. But perhaps, aye, better than facing this.

"No," I said.

She turned and looked at me, victory in her eyes. "RapAnn, you are far too ready to use that word. Despite that—via the mercy you crave, yet do not deserve—I grant you still another chance to give me your answer. Will you accept Master Cole?"

"No," I repeated.

"Then here you shall stay, until I come and ask you again."

"There is no way in."

She laughed. "No," she agreed, "nor out."

Chapter Eight

And so my true imprisonment began. In the stories they tell of me, aye, there is always a tower, and it is guarded round by magic. So it was. In the tales, there is no door, and the witch places me there in order to protect me.

But nay, she did it to break me.

I do not know aught of my ancestors, what ilk of people they were, save that my parents were thieves. Peasants all, they must have been. Aye, and they must have had some mettle, for whatever I'd inherited stood me well in the days that followed.

My prison consisted of but a single room, round and with bare stone walls. It was indeed attended by magic. Had I ever doubted Lady Margaret's powers, I ceased to do so then. For she transported me into the tower using only magic, there being no door, as said. And a very short while later, she and both her guards departed.

Leaving me alone.

I'd imagined myself lonely before, aye, but this felt far different. At the manor house, even though shut away from everyone, I'd been able to sense life all around me. The house itself lived. This stone tower did not. Cold, dead stone it was. It seemed to give off its own penetrating cold, even though a fire burned in the middle of the floor.

About that fire—like the one she'd once kindled on the empty stones of the hearth in my room, this too burned by magic, having no fuel and springing up right from the bare slates. The spell ensured that it never burned down. Neither did the flames flare up.

The fire gave off only moderate heat, nothing sufficient to battle the pervasive chill. Other than that, the furnishings were few. Three gowns hung against the wall, all in a row. All of them were made of plain homespun, blue with braided belts. There was a narrow cot with a single blanket, and one three-legged stool.

No books. No candles. Not a single instrument upon which to make music or otherwise amuse myself. Only the silence.

How can I describe that silence? Deep, and fathomless—it seemed to reach beyond the window and stretch away into forever.

In truth, there were sounds outside the window, which stood open when we arrived, though it was equipped with shutters which I supposed might be closed from within, against the weather. The trees, whose tops from this height were at eye-level, tossed their branches in the wind, and the air whistled around the stones.

Nothing else. No sight or sound of another human or animal.

Even on that first day, as evening swiftly descended, I realized how important that window would be. There was nothing else, no focal point. Inside the room I had only the cot, the stool, those three gowns, a comb for my hair, and a cramped garderobe.

Outside lay the world. A wild world, aye, but better than nothing.

When the dark came down that first night, though, I felt afraid. I spotted dark shapes in flight outside, and feared they might come in through the window. So I closed the shutters. But then there was no light at all, save the low glimmer of the fire, and the interior of the tower felt like a tomb. I settled for leaving one leaf of the shutters open a crack.

Then I changed into one of the gowns—warmer than my own rags—dragged the cot nearer the fire, and tried to sleep.

It must have taken me hours to drop off. I lay on the uncomfortable cot trying to imagine what my life had become, and how I might survive.

If I could not bear the silence, could not bear the loneliness, I supposed I might cast myself from the window. The drop—a dizzying distance—would surely kill me. All my troubles would end.

Yet it seemed cowardly to contemplate it. After all my resistance and my defiance of Lady Margaret, would I truly allow her to win?

My customary answer came to my lips and I spoke it aloud to the chamber. "No."

I awoke sometime later, to music. For a terrifying moment, I didn't know where I was. Then I saw the lighter darkness beyond the cracked shutter, and heard—

A song.

It rose and fell in a beautiful cadence like the voice of a young girl. Indeed, the high pitch of it suggested not only youth but sweetness.

I sat there in the dark chamber with my loosened hair all around me, my heart pounding fit to beat out of my chest.

The song stopped and started. I wondered if it might be magical, if Lady Margaret had left it to comfort me. But when had she ever done aught to comfort me?

I do not know how long it took me to realize the truth, that what I heard was but the wind coming in through the wooden shutter I'd left ajar.

But what is truth? Did the wind not produce a song, and did that song not serve to comfort me? Was it not, then, the wind's voice?

One cannot see the wind. I got up and padded across to the window, where I hesitated to touch the shutter lest I destroy the song. The air coming in felt very cold. Through the narrow opening I could see just a glimpse of stars.

I whispered to the wind, "Will you be my companion?" The answer might as well have been my own constant reply to Lady Margaret—no. For after that first night, I was never able—try as I might—to set the shutter to produce another song. Perhaps the wind needed to be just right, or the angle. Night after night, day after day I tried, to no effect.

How to describe my life there in the tower, or how difficult I found adjustment to it? Looking back now, it seems a blur. Yet that is the meat of the story that is told of me, is it not? A maid in a tower, one with fantastically long hair.

There is truth in some stories; others, I suppose, are fabrications and lies. Some quite likely tangle the two together. I seemed to be alone in that place, hideously alone, and guarded round by magic.

But was I truly alone? If so, to whose thoughts did I listen? To whom did I speak aloud—for such, after the first few days, I did. I spoke to an unseen companion, to the wind and to the stones themselves. To the fire, which burned soundlessly. I listened for answers.

I think I must have gone a little mad those first days, those first weeks. I had lost everything for which I cared. My home of a lifetime. My books, my familiar possessions, worst of all my beautiful musical instruments.

Let me tell you, that is a bitter thing to bear. It leaves one bereft as a twisted piece of driftwood cast up on the shore. We anchor ourselves by the things we love, the things we know.

All gone.

In their place I had the three gowns—each identical to the others, so I did not know which one I wore on any given day. That might not seem important, yet it was. I craved variety the way I'd once craved pastry squares.

Speaking of food, Lady Margaret had left me a supply—a pot of porridge, a loaf of bread, and a bowl of currants. These, like the jug of water I found with them on a shelf, and like the fire, magically renewed themselves. If I ate half the loaf, or a handful of currants, a short while later they would reappear—just the same amount, never more and never less.

I am not particularly fond of porridge. And I feared eating magical food, for its effect on me. But hunger is a powerful motivator. I managed to choke down some porridge by sprinkling it with currants, which I did like. Not good fare, but it kept me alive.

At first, I counted the days, though in my madness I fear I lost track. There was nothing to do. Never underestimate the torture of that. One might suppose it pleasant to be free of work, but the mind requires occupation, or at least mine did.

As I'd guessed it would, the window became the focus of my world. I would sit there despite the cold, gazing out at what little I could see, though even that swiftly took on a measure of sameness, trees as far as the eye could reach, now bare of leaves. A gap of perhaps twenty or thirty paces lay between the trees and the bottom of the tower—believe me, I estimated it again and again—where lay rough grass mostly covered by snow.

The view never changed. But the trees, so I reasoned, were alive. So I spoke to them. After a while, I fancied they answered me. They signaled their replies by tossing their branches and, on rare occasions, they too sang songs.

I asked them, "When will Lady Margaret return?" I half dreaded and half hoped she would. This was but part of the old game—she sought to soften me before she came and asked the eternal question once more.

To which I would reply no.

Though I did long to return to the manor house. You may think it strange I should wish to go back to that existence, also that of a prisoner, but it felt far more known, more comfortable than this.

The old thought once again began chasing its way around in my head. Would it be so bad to accept Master Cole's protection? At least then I could go home. I would be given a new room, aye, but I had no doubt it would be comfortable and warm. I would be given beautiful gowns and delightful delicacies to eat.

But the price for all that—ah, the price! Submitting to Jeremiah Cole, allowing him to touch me…

I did not expect Lady Margaret to return until after her grand Solstice celebration, and I could only guess when that might take place. When she did come, aye, I would give her my customary answer.

Or would I?

Aye, indeed, I once more came close to breaking. A single thought saved me: an idea.

I awoke one morning from troubling dreams. I'd been dreaming more and more, perhaps as an escape, perhaps encouraged by all the magic that surrounded me. This time I thought I heard the notes I'd once plucked on strings—as if I were safe back in my chamber at the manor house, with my harp in my hands. Antony sat opposite me, giving me a lesson, admiration shining clear in his eyes. The notes I plucked served as a balm; they soothed my heart. But then the harp came apart in my hands, fell to pieces as it had when Lady Margaret smashed it. And Antony crumbled to dust, which blew away.

I had lost all. I came awake with that thought repeating in my mind. If only I might have even one instrument restored to me…

Then I realized I had one still. The same as that of the trees and the shutter.

I had my voice.

Climbing from my narrow cot, I went to the window. Dawn broke across the tops of the trees, bleeding rosy radiance. The cold felt bitter, but that scarcely mattered.

Lady Margaret could not stop me singing, not unless she silenced me for good. And the songs this instrument might produce were infinite.

There in the cold dawn, I wept for joy.

Chapter Nine

Thereafter, I sang. I trilled and warbled like a bird, of which I saw none. I serenaded the trees and sang my thoughts aloud to myself, even the mundane ones. I addressed melodies to the fire, and to the stars at night.

A great comfort, it seemed to draw the world closer to me. The stars actually leaned nearer, as if to listen; the trees rustled in response to my voice. Hearing my songs, they became part of me.

Strangely, in the past my voice had never been my chosen instrument. Too many others clamored for my attention, such as the harpsichord and the viol. I had, of course, been given voice lessons, but never thought much of my ability.

Now it became everything to me. I sang the songs I knew and made up many others. At night, they wound through my head and through my sleep.

My favored occupation became sitting in the window and singing while combing out my hair, the comb being one of my few possessions. Lacking Elsie's care, my hair had once more grown tangled. But I worked at it, combing out those knots with long strokes in rhythm with the music.

Time passed.

How much time, I could not truly say, for I had once more lost track of it. Later I thought I should have scratched a mark on the wall for each day of my captivity. But I did not, and they slipped away in a blur, ruled mostly by the weather. When storms came, I had foreknowledge, for I could see them moving in from miles across the sky. Then I would be forced to close the shutters and lie on my cot listening, with only the fire for light and company. I sang soft, sad laments. And at those times I wondered about the future, whether my existence would always be this, one of unending endurance.

It did not remain thus. Some weeks after the winter Solstice, by my best guess, Lady Margaret returned.

I heard them coming, first of all. So great was my silence, I could hear everything for miles, and the ground being iron hard, the horses' hooves rang.

Of course, the carriage could not make it all the way through the forest. As before, Lady Margaret accomplished the last part of the journey on foot, trailed by her attendants. I watched from the window, unable to tear myself away.

And oh, how the sight of her affected me! I'd been lonely in the tower, true—half mad with loneliness. But as I now discovered, there had been a measure of peace in my isolation. For the first time ever, I was out from under Lady Margaret's eye.

No more. She brought all the emotions back with her—doubt, fear and dread. She paused at the bottom of the tower and stood gazing up at the window, looking every inch the queen—nay, every inch the witch. Clad all in dark green, a shade so deep it almost appeared black, with a cloak that swept the surface of the snow, she glowed with confidence, and the very sight of her knocked me back on my heels.

"RapAnn," she called. "Can you hear me?"

She must have seen me peering around the edge of the stone casement while I pondered what to do. A thousand thoughts pounded through my head.

Had she come to take me home? Had my sentence been served?

Did I want to go with her?

Of course, of course I did. I wanted to feel the life of the manor all around me, to catch glimpses, out other windows, of those who were supposedly my family. To eat something besides porridge, currants, and bread.

To exchange one prison for another.

"RapAnn!" she called again.

Oh, the power of her! It made me show myself—stand fully revealed—and look down, all the way down, at her.

How beautiful she looked, her cruel face perfect as a work of art.

She smiled at me. "I half expected to find you here at the bottom of the tower, broken on the stones. Pull me up."

Pull her up? Whatever did she mean?

The guards had backed off—not far—and stood with their swords drawn. Did they expect me to attack her? I would, if I could. But if I found a way to kill her, would her magic die with her? Without the fire and food, I would also die.

Last time, when the two of us first arrived here, she had transported me inside by magic. She might well have transported herself in now, I supposed. Instead she made an impatient gesture.

"Stupid girl! There—the hook."

I looked where she indicated. On the left side of the window, well embedded in the stone, was a stout hook.

I'd noticed it before, of course—I'd noticed everything in my prison—but had never thought it more than a possible anchor for the shutters.

"Let down your hair!" she cried.

I could not have heard her right. I gaped at her, stupid in truth.

"Wind your hair around the hook and let it down. I shall climb."

Even when I comprehended it, I did not want to obey. It felt, somehow, humiliating—no doubt precisely what she intended—and anyway, I did not want her inside with me. Moreover, I did not believe my hair would hold her weight. Long as it was, it could not possibly reach the ground. And how could she climb it without causing me pain?

Yet such was her power, her command, I gathered up the length of the tresses, bundled them together, and slung them over the iron hook. My hair was not quite long enough. She must have used magic to reach, for she extended an arm and snagged the end of the golden hair rope.

When she pulled on it, it did not hurt. The hook took all the pressure, and she came easily over the sill to stand beside me.

I unwound my hair from the hook and we stood gazing at one another.

Fear is a curious thing. I had feared her, in one way or another, all my life. Imprisoned as I'd been these many weeks, I had at least been free of that emotion, but it came rushing back upon me now with sickening force.

"Well, girl?" she said with a hint of challenge, as if she expected me to throw myself at her feet, to weep and beg for rescue from my high cell. "How do you find your confinement?"

How did I find it? As if I would speak to her of the shattering loneliness, the dark hours when I'd held myself tight. The glorious afternoons spent singing. I'd learned more guile than that.

"It is the same as ever," I said.

She did not like that answer, no. She wanted me broken. I saw the rage that flashed through her eyes.

Tearing her gaze from mine, she glanced around the chamber. "You have little enough here."

"True, my lady."

Perhaps she'd come to take from me, again. But, what might she take? My clothing? My blanket?

"Master Cole sends his greetings. He hopes you are well, and despite all your defiance, he holds out a welcome to you. A special chamber has been prepared, just as I promised. It contains every comfort. Lovely gowns in which you may accompany him to all the grand events. A large, luxurious bed. Your musical instruments are already there. You need only say yes."

The one word I could not utter. Not to her. I wondered again about the nature of truth. She said she came on Master Cole's behalf, but I thought it was on her own. She could not stand anyone defying her. So simple, and so profound.

So she spoke lies. She made omissions. The luxurious bed would contain Master Cole. I preferred the narrow cot.

I said nothing. Only a few slender rules of magic protected me—I dared not risk violating them.

"He would like you at his side for the next great event, the Spring Equinox. I bid you give me your answer, RapAnn. But beware—if I leave you here now, I will not soon return. If you miss this chance to escape, you will not soon be offered another. Your imprisonment will be a long one."

I contemplated that. Already it seemed long, yet it had been mere weeks. Could I endure longer? I wanted to ask her how long she meant to leave me but dared not show such weakness.

Instead I lifted my chin and said, "I am well enough."

She hissed like a snake. "Foolish chit."

"Pray, bid Master Cole find another upon whom he may center his attentions." And unleash his doubtless vile appetites.

Her eyes gleamed with rage. "And if I forget you here? If I go away and never return?"

"My lady, you have done a fine job of teaching me endurance."

"Aye, then." She spat the words at me, quick as the sting of a wasp. "We shall discover of what your endurance is made."

Chapter Ten

I endured. The long winter turned to spring, the trees budded before my eyes and leafed out into clouds of green. How beautiful my bower then! And how heartfelt the songs elicited from me.

Birds came. Imagine my delight when the first of them arrived and nested among the new leaves. No longer alone, I sang to them, and I fancied they twittered and chirped in reply to my songs. They darted back and forth among the trees, making bright flickers of color, and wooed one another endlessly.

Oh, how I rejoiced in their presence! The forest beyond my window, once so silent, came alive.

One day, at the end of spring it must have been, I heard a commotion from far off and feared—hoped—Lady Margaret might be returning. I watched and watched, and thought I heard a troop of horse ride by, but I saw no one. Had folk on horseback merely passed through the wood? Might they come here and catch sight of me?

Might I, in fact, be rescued?

Until then, I'd given no credence to that possibility. Now it obsessed my mind. I spent every waking moment seated on my three-legged stool at the window, and strained my ears. But no one came near.

My hair, to which I gave so much attention, continued to grow. It seemed to do so magically, and soon pooled at my feet. For ease of movement, I kept it braided most the time in a thick golden rope.

My loneliness, slightly alleviated by the presence of the birds, continued until the end of summer, when another visitor arrived.

Like the lady and her guards, it came preceded by noise—in this case a very great disturbance. Crashing twigs and branches brought me to the window, just in time to see all the resident birds fly up, startled. A creature dashed into the clearing that surrounded the tower.

You will be surprised to hear I did not know what it was. I'd seen animals on Lady Margaret's estate—there were mice and cats in the garden. The horses, of course. Dogs and cattle.

This looked like none of those. Large, squat and powerful, it had great, hunched shoulders and tapered flanks, and tusks set either side of an aggressive snout. It took a stand, facing back the way it had come, and snorted loudly.

Whatever this was, something or someone else pursued it. I heard more sounds, swiftly approaching, from the distance.

Hunters, I thought. I could not identify this creature, yet someone came after it. I began to hope then, in a blinding burst. Let them follow it here. Let them see me, and rescue me.

But it did not happen that way. The snorting beast stood at bay for several long moments before moving around the side of the tower, where it disappeared from my sight. It never even glanced at the tower, or me. All sounds of pursuit died away.

The occurrence shook me. I'd once fancied Lady

Margaret must guard this place around with magic, to keep everyone away. Was it not so?

Winter lay ahead—long and sharp, and lonely. How could I endure it?

If anyone should come to rescue me, I reasoned, it must be now.

And then, aye—like an answer to my thoughts, he did come.

****

I'd been up since first light, sitting by the window, combing my hair and singing, singing… For a time, the birds came to listen. A pair of redbirds had made their nest in one of the trees directly opposite my window, and occasionally while I sang they swooped past, beaks opened as if joining in the chorus.

I decided to make a song for them, and incorporated their own trill into it, sweet and high. I laughed when it encouraged them to swoop closer.

I swear, so caught up was I in the music, I failed to hear anyone approach. Or perhaps he made no sound. For he came very gently, picking his way.

And suddenly, he just appeared in the clearing, directly opposite my window.

For an instant, I did not believe the evidence of my eyes. Even given the occurrence of the strange, fierce animal only days ago, I thought this an illusion. But such a fine one!

A young man it was, all clad in hunting leathers. He had brown hair that gleamed with hints of copper in the sun. It lay smooth upon his bare head, long enough to brush his collar and slightly sweated, as if he'd had a hard tramp, or ride. A hunter, no doubt, out after a beast such as that which had invaded the clearing.

Aye, for along with the hunting jacket of dark green, the brown leggings and tall leather boots, he wore a quiver of arrows slung across his back.

He lifted his face toward mine, and I felt a thrill. *He saw me.* Someone, at last, saw me! The way he cocked his ear argued he'd also heard me.

He had heard me singing.

Emotion poured over me—fear, doubt, and victorious joy. Singing was the most intimate thing I ever did, and he had heard, *he had heard.* Heat rushed through me in a wave, and for an instant I wanted to hide. But how could I? Out of nowhere had come possible salvation.

Or terrible danger.

He came closer, walking like a man in a trance. He still moved without a sound, making me wonder again—was he really here, or had Lady Margaret sent a spell to beguile and somehow trick me?

I truly should withdraw into the tower and hide myself. Yet I stood with the comb in one hand, the other resting on the stone sill.

Do we know at once, when we meet with our destiny? Do we recognize the truth, when it comes? Or is truth never so easily seen?

"Fair maiden!" he called up to me. He had a melodious voice and a heavy brogue. It had been so long since I'd heard any voice other than my own and the birds' that I trembled where I stood.

"Do no' be frightened. I but heard ye singing— from afar off, I did—and followed the sound. 'Twas the most heavenly thing ever to meet my ears."

Finer than the songs of the birds? Than the wind in the trees? Than a viol or the sweet notes plucked from a harp? Surely not.

"Who are you? How come ye here?"

I scarcely knew how to reply. I did not doubt a name had power, especially mine, bestowed like a punishment.

He stole still closer, moving with lithe grace and eagerness.

"I can see no way into the tower, good maiden. Is the door on the other side?"

I shook my head. No door. No way in, or out.

"Are ye a prisoner?"

Ah, now there was a question. What if I confessed that I was? What would he do?

Not satisfied with my response, he walked back and forth several paces, inspecting the tower all around its base, no doubt searching for the nonexistent entry, before he called up to me, "Can ye no' speak? Aye, but ye must—I heard ye singing."

"I can speak," I replied.

"Then tell me, what is this place? I swear, I never knew 'twas here, even though this land borders that o' my father, and we do hunt nearby."

"Was that you, hunting the other day?" I asked. "I heard you, and saw a beast, a great tusked beast."

"The boar. Aye, he is ancient and wily, and we ha' yet to bring him down. I sometimes doubt we ever will."

He continued looking up at me, straining to see. "Can ye no' come down, mistress, and let me in? I can espy no way in or out."

"There is no way, and I cannot come down."

He breathed a word I did not catch. "How d'ye come there, then?"

"Magic."

"Ah."

"Have you—have you heard of a woman called Lady Margaret Beddor?"

"Lady Margaret Beddor? The witch? To be sure."

That would put him off. It would send him hastening back through the wood to find his horse and ride away as swiftly as possible.

"All ha' heard o' her," he assured me. "And none eager to cross her."

"It is she has built this tower as my prison, and shut me in."

He did not turn away, did not leave. Neither did he appear particularly intimidated by the information.

"For what crime?" he called.

I did not answer.

"Lass, why has she imprisoned ye?"

"Return to your horse and your hunt. Save yourself."

"Is there some magical door, one I cannot see?" Once again, he circled the tower, as if searching.

"No door," I reiterated when he reappeared.

"Are there guards?"

"None." But she would know he'd been here. Somehow, I believed, she would. She knew everything.

"How do ye get food and water in and out?"

"I do not."

"How d'ye live, then? There maun be a way."

It occurred to me I could let down my hair for him. The shocking thought, which seemed even more intimate than his having heard me sing, fair shook me to the core. No one ever touched me, save Lady Margaret and Elsie—and Jeremiah Cole once when he had touched my hand.

That memory made me shudder. But the thought of this young man touching my hair affected me in a far different manner.

If I let my hair down for him, would he climb up? Should I? If we stood face to face with one another, what would happen then? Would it be wise, would it start something wonderful or something very terrible indeed?

"What is your name?" he called up.

"RapAnn."

"'Tis a strange name, that one."

"There is a reason for it."

"A story, no doubt. I am Prince Kenzie MacAlver, of the Fife Kingdom. And I am sworn to rescue any maid in distress."

A prince? Ah, surely I lay asleep in my cot, dreaming. Outside of stories, such encounters did not occur.

Yet it did not help me decide what to do. Never, since the day I was born, had I possessed much say in my destiny. Now I closed my eyes an instant before I took it into my own hands.

I told him, "I do know of a way you may be able to come in."

Chapter Eleven

So seldom do desire and wisdom go hand in hand.
This thing, I had learned. My mother desired the tender
rape that grew in Lady Margaret's garden. My father,
presumably, desired to please her, and so he stole from
that garden, failing to heed the wisdom that advised
against crossing his mistress. When caught, he desired
to save his own neck and so traded me away, not
heeding what might become of me then.

I likewise knew it the height of foolishness to cross
Lady Margaret now. True, she remained far away, but
as stated, I believed she would find out if I violated the
sanctity of my prison by admitting this young man. She
sustained the place—provided me with food, water, and
fire—by her magic. Reason dictated she could well halt
such provisions, were the tower breeched.

But I desired...not rescue so much, for I did not
believe in rescue then. But company. Indeed, my very
spirit cried out for just a few moments with someone,
even if naught more came of it.

In the beginning, the prince balked at the prospect
of climbing up my hair. He feared hurting me, even
after I showed him how I might sling the length of the
tresses over the iron hook and relieve the tension on my
head.

"Look—the braid is like a rope."

"This is the only way in?"

"This, or magic."

He tugged on the yellow braid gingerly. Then he swarmed up it, using his feet against the stones to climb. Up he came, and over the sill.

Into my life.

And oh, he made the room so small! Large he seemed, in that confined, circular space. I could smell him at once. He smelled of sunshine and horse, and something else that must have been sweat.

Hastily, I unhooked my braid and backed off.

He held out his hands. "Peace, mistress. I'll not harm you."

I looked into his face, and he into mine, the first real opportunity we'd had, given the previous distance.

He was not handsome, not like some of Lady Margaret's guests who, though men, might be deemed pretty. He had a broad forehead, browned by the sun, and an angular jaw—almost square—covered by a trace of beard. His nose, being straight, lent little character. But his eyes—och, his eyes. Earnest and brown, they regarded me from between thick, dark lashes. Gazing into them, I breathed more easily, for I knew he would never hurt me, not by intention.

"Mistress RapAnn." He sketched a courtly bow and I dropped a curtsy, as I'd been taught. Ridiculous, perhaps, for us to be standing in my tower prison, performing such civilized niceties.

"Prince Kenzie, I am happy to make your acquaintance." Happy, yes.

"The pleasure is all mine."

He seemed as unable to look away from my face as I was reluctant to look away from his. But he shot a glance around the room.

"What is this place? Is this the sole chamber?"

"The only one, yes."

"The fire—it burns with no fuel."

"As I said, it is magic. The fire burns eternally."

"Magic. I—I see."

"'Tis the same with the food and water. I eat and drink, and they are restored. Never more, never less."

"By God! How long have you been here?"

"Since before the last winter solstice."

"So long! And your jailer—does she return?"

"She does. Not often, but she seeks an answer from me, one I refuse to give."

He cursed softly and regarded me again. "A wonder you ha' not gone mad. What do you do, to pass the time?"

"I sing."

He brightened immediately. "Aye, I heard your song. It led me here. List to me, Mistress RapAnn—it did feel as if I were being led, as if I were meant to find you here. I see that I must free you from this place."

"I doubt you can."

"Of course I can."

"It is far too dangerous. She—Lady Margaret will know."

"She is not here, this dread Lady Margaret."

"It doesn't matter. She will know."

He waved a hand. "If you suppose I will leave ye here to languish in this—this blighted cell, you are very much mistaken."

My heart rose. Nay, it bounded.

"There is no way."

"'Tis the easiest of things, mistress. I have only to go away and return wi' a length of rope. This we will tie to yon hook in place of your hair. Then we both may climb down."

Could it truly be so simple? And then, what after that? I knew so little of the world. Just the tiny bits Lady Margaret permitted me to see, and what I could glimpse through my windows both at the manor house and here.

I knew nothing of life. I found the prospect of freedom terrifying.

"No," I breathed.

"Aye, mistress. But first you must sit down wi' me and tell me all. How you fell into the witch's power, and what question she would ha' you answer."

Dared I? I'd never confided in anyone. Not in Elsie, certainly not in Master Cole. There had been no one else.

And he—Prince Kenzie—was so unlike anyone I'd ever met. As I say, most the men among Lady Margaret's company were, with the exception of the guards, pale and fancy as peacocks, slightly effete. Prince Kenzie—well, he looked plain and steady and honest.

Had I ever before gazed into a pair of truly honest eyes?

"Very well," I said. "I will tell you all. And when you have heard the tale, then you shall make up your mind as to whether or not you still wish to try and help me."

****

The tale took a goodly time to tell. I recited it like someone else's story, one perhaps stolen from one of my old books. Like the tale that is told of me.

He listened. I will say this of him, he did so

patiently, with very few interruptions, only a faint exclamation now and again, and the clenching of his fists.

I interrupted myself only to fetch us water when my voice grew hoarse. We drank from the same—my only—cup.

As I spoke, the light faded from the sky and the birds settled back into the trees. If he worried for the welfare of his horse, presumably left back in the forest, like Lady Margaret's carriage when she came, he gave no indication. Night came on.

"And so," Kenzie said at last, when the tale played out, like the length of my hair, "she has deprived you of one thing after another, even your freedom, in an effort to make you accept this man?"

"She has taken all from me."

"Your courage astounds me. I ha' known a wealth o' brave men in my time, including my elder brothers and my father, the king. But their deeds pale in comparison wi' what you ha' endured."

"It is kind in you to say."

"No kindness, mistress, but truth."

"I do not understand the truth. I fear I have never heard much of it."

"The truth is, you are as courageous as you are beautiful." He caught my fingers in his and raised them to his lips. In the same motion, he fell from his place on the windowsill where he'd been perched all the while, to one knee.

"Allow me, Mistress RapAnn, to be your champion and your savior. Grant to me that great privilege."

Oh, the feel of his lips, warm and sure, on my fingers! It made my head go light. But I could not permit this.

"Have you not heard what I've told you?" I cried.

"Aye, I have." He did not release my hand.

"Lady Margaret is powerful. She is wicked. If you take me from here, she will make you pay for it."

"How will she know?"

"She will. She will!"

"It is many a mile to her manor, and you say she comes but seldom. Even if her magic allows her to tell you have escaped, we will be long gone by the time she reaches here. Down the rope and awa'."

"She will find out. She will pursue you to the end of the earth. To the end of your life."

"She may well try. Trust me, RapAnn, I will keep you safe."

It was not for my safety I feared. Bitterly, I told him, "You would have done better had you never heard my song or seen this tower."

"It is not so." He cradled my hand in both of his. "Pray, let me rescue you."

"And what after that?"

"I shall tak' ye home wi' me, is what. To my father and brothers, who will help protect you from her. You shall ha' a stout castle and stalwart guards all 'round."

Slowly, I shook my head. What would his father—the king of Fife—think of him bringing home the daughter of a thief? And no, there was no possible protection from Lady Margaret—that I believed to my very bones.

He leaped to his feet. "You can tell me nay. But ye canna' expect me to leave ye here. Knowing you remain a prisoner will haunt me. 'Tis more than I can bear."

"You do not know her," I whispered, "nor the extent of her cruelty." I turned my fingers in his and clasped them tight. "Go away from here, yes. Spare yourself the grief that must come. Forget you ever saw me."

"Forget?" He inspected my face once more, his gaze warm enough to melt me clear through. "One thing I will ne'er do is forget."

Chapter Twelve

Kenzie climbed back through the window and down the rope of my hair in near darkness, only the stars and the trees witnessing his descent. Before he left, he dug in his pocket and produced a small treasure—an apple, the first I'd seen in many months—which he tossed back up to me.

"Here, a change from the sameness o' your diet. 'Tis a bit bashed about after the ride, but I will bring more when I return."

I leaned down from the casement, having unwound my braid from the hook. "You are certain you wish to return?"

"I am."

"When might I expect you?"

"Tomorrow, so I do promise." He made a bow. "Trust me, Mistress RapAnn."

I listened to him move into the wood and, at length, ride off through the soft, new dark, wondering, wondering—had it been but a dream? Did I perhaps lie abed, the victim of fever?

Was I dying?

But no. I stood on my two feet. And with him gone, the little room seemed the same as ever. Yet I held the apple in my hand.

Proof, was it not?

He had not lied; the apple had shriveled slightly in

his pocket. I did not care; I ate it anyway, with more relish than I'd employed over any food in a year.

Oh, how the sweetness of it lingered on my tongue. The memory of Kenzie lingered likewise in my mind, equally sweet despite my misgivings.

Those misgivings may well be imagined. Me, risking my safety through my continued defiance of Lady Margaret, was one thing. Endangering he who had come to me like a miracle, that was something else again.

I slept little that night. I had set the apple core on the windowsill—as proof, mayhap—but during the night a wind came up and swept it off.

By morning, rain moved in. I kept the shutters open anyway and looked out often, straining for a glimpse of anything moving among the trees, despite the rain.

I did not know how far he had to travel. Lady Margaret's lands were vast. He'd said they bordered his father's kingdom, a kingdom that was quite likely also large. I lectured myself to patience, but oh, it proved hard.

I had made up my mind he'd never existed or, if he had, he'd thought better of arraying his family against Lady Margaret by rescuing me.

But in the middle of the afternoon, I heard a cry.

"RapAnn, RapAnn! Let down your hair."

I flew to the casement and leaned out dangerously far, so the rain drenched me.

There he stood, wearing a brown leather cloak this time, and with a bundle tucked beneath one arm. He waved a hand at me through the rain, and I hurried to wind my hair, already braided, around the hook. With trembling hands, I let it snake down outside the stones.

Kenzie climbed up swiftly, using the toes of his boots between the stones, as he had before. Shedding water, he crossed the sill onto the floor.

"Oh," I exclaimed. "Oh, I did not think you would return."

"I did promise, RapAnn. I promised." He reached out and, quite simply, drew me into his arms, where he clutched me fiercely before letting me go with a rueful laugh. "Forgive me—I've got you all wet."

"It does not matter, if—if I'm to leave."

"I brought a stout bit o' rope." He wore it slung over one shoulder. "Pack up what you wish to take and let us awa' while we ha' the light."

"There is naught for me to take. I have not even a cloak."

"Take mine." He unslung the rope and unfurled the leather cloak from his shoulders before placing it about me.

"I can use the blanket," I tried to tell him.

"Leave it. Leave everything from this awful place. Here, only let me secure the rope to the hook, and we will away."

I could scarce believe it. I fell back out of his way as he uncoiled the rope and leaned one knee on the embrasure to secure it to the hook at the left side. The rain lashed in, and the wind shivered the shutters beside him.

I thought, at first, that was what took him so long, the wind interfering with his task. He cursed softly, with what sounded like growing frustration.

"What is it?" I started forward. "What is amiss?"

He answered over his shoulder, hands still busy, "The accursed rope will not tie to the hook. Look!"

I pressed in beside him, thoughtlessly close.

"No matter how I try to secure it to the hook, it merely unloops. See?"

I did, and my heart sank impossibly. The rope seemed to have a mind of its own. Each time Kenzie tied it, the loops slunk away again, as if repelled by the iron.

"Is somewhat wrong with the rope?" I asked, though I knew the truth, even then.

"Nay, 'tis good and stout, this, the best and longest I could find. I do no' understand it."

"Magic," I breathed.

"Eh?" He turned his head and his eyes, wide and filled with chagrin, met mine.

"It is part of how she protects this place. That hook will be enchanted to hold naught but my hair." I seized hold of him with both hands. "You must leave here at once. Get away now, before she finds out, before she comes."

"If you think I will leave you here, you are very much mistaken."

"You must. You must!" I wept the words. You can only imagine my feelings. I'd hoped I might be able to leave this prison at last, and my disappointment fair sickened me.

"There, now. Do no' weep." He drew me once more into his arms, there in the open casement. The rain lashed at us, and the storm of my tears matched it.

"There, lass, it will be all right. We will find another way."

"How? I am trapped. At her mercy forever. Only, she has no mercy."

He comforted me as best he could with his hands

on my hair.

"I shall not let her keep you, RapAnn—and neither shall that beast she calls 'friend' have you."

"But I cannot leave."

"And I will no' leave you. Not like this, not this night. Lass, look at me."

I lifted my head from his chest and, once more, we gazed into each other's eyes. I felt the strength of him take hold inside me, equal parts wondrous and frightening.

"Prince Kenzie, you have done your best to keep your promise. No shame to you, her magic is so strong. You'd best leave, now."

"Hush. Did I no' promise to sustain you in any way I might? I will no' leave you alone here."

I didn't argue it further. How could I, shattered as I was? Instead I clutched at him with desperate hands and let him hold me all that night long.

For we spent that night in the same cot, which proved much too small for the purpose. In truth, Kenzie lay on the cot and I lay atop him, both of us beneath his leather cloak for warmth.

And how warm it was!

He'd climbed down just before dark, using the rope of my hair, and tended his horse, sheltering it as near as he could to the tower, in the forest. Thereafter we closed the shutters and, with only the fire for light, passed the night.

The first night within my memory I had not spent alone. Can I express how much comfort I found? Though nothing passed between us beyond a warm embrace, by morning I felt I knew him. And I trusted him as I never had anyone else.

The rain had passed during the night, and the day dawned clear. Kenzie had brought food in his pack, which he insisted I eat while he used his dagger to shred my blanket into strips, which he in turn twined into a rope, his thinking being that the hook might not reject something already a part of the enchantment.

But after all that effort, when he tried to attach the blanket rope to the iron hook, it held no better than had the line he'd brought with him.

I will admit, despair touched me then. I wanted away, and I wanted to leave with him. There seemed no hope for me—something he must now grasp in full. He would surely desert me.

Indeed, he gazed at me so gravely, and with such a somber expression in his eyes, I felt sure he sought a way to break that very news to me.

He began, "RapAnn"—for we'd dropped Mistress and Prince during the closely spent night—"I shall have to use your hair to climb down."

"Yes, I understand." I would not weep again. I did not wish him to remember me as a sniveling child, when he had expressed such admiration for my courage. I did not feel courageous now.

"I need to ride back home. There I will consult wi' a friend who knows much about magic. He may know of a way to break this cruel spell."

"You can tell no one else about me. Should she find out, I do not know what she will do." Abandoned here at her mercy, I had no hope.

"But, lass, there maun be a way—"

I gazed at him steadily where he stood with his back to the window, surrounded by morning light. So many things I wished to say, but the pain of losing him prevented any of it passing my lips.

He seemed to read my thoughts, though, in my eyes. "Lass, I do no' abandon ye. I will return. We will find a way to get you free from this tower, and from Lady Margaret's power, both."

I did not believe there was a way. But I asked, "And once I am free?"

"As I have said, I shall take ye back to my father's kingdom wi' me. But—there is somewhat ye should know. I am not at liberty to take ye for wife, for I am betrothed already. 'Twas a match arranged many years ago, and her father is an ally o' my own, from a northern kingdom. I do no' love her." He continued gazing at me steadily. "I do no' think I guessed what love is, till now. But my father's word has been given on it, and I am bound."

"Oh." I did not expect him to confide in me. Certainly he owed me nothing, and once he rode away from here, having failed to rescue me, I did not expect ever to see him again.

Despite his promise. For promises are based on truth, and I'd had so little of that, in my life.

When I said nothing more, he went on, the words bursting from him, "Were it not so, were I no' betrothed to Lady Anastacia, I would take ye home wi' me and wed wi' ye myself, and keep ye safe for a lifetime."

An impossible outcome—one that might appear in some book of fanciful tales. I knew, all too well, life is not a fairy tale. It is hard and unjust and, miracles are few.

Nonexistent, for me—despite the fact that he'd appeared to be a miracle when first he strode into the clearing.

"I am sorry." Compassion flooded his brown eyes, along with another emotion I could not so easily identify. "But it will no' keep me away, RapAnn. I will consult wi' Justin, as I say, and when I return, I will bring all I can, including food and some books. Is there aught else you require?"

"A—a musical instrument, please." If he came.

"One other than your lovely voice?" He took me in his arms and kissed me, lips on lips. I'd never been touched that way, despite how we'd spent the previous night. I might have taken it as a salute, a thing bestowed as a mark of affection the way a brother might, to a sister. Except I felt far too much warmth in it, a current running deep that seemed to bind us one to the other.

"I will return," he repeated, when he removed his lips from mine.

But not even that kiss convinced me he would.

Chapter Thirteen

Oh, how difficult I found being alone after sharing Kenzie's company, even for just one night. I suffered as if my heart had been torn out of my chest by the roots. The birds seemed to flash by my window less brightly, and the songs died in my throat.

I relived every word he'd spoken to me, a score of times over. I recalled his every movement, every expression. I yearned as I never had before.

Fiercely, I attempted to school myself in the face of such feelings, to protect myself from knowing that he would not—should not—return. Indeed, he'd promised he would, and I believed he'd meant it. He seemed a sincere and honest man withal. But when I looked at it fairly, why would he risk his safety for a stranger?

I sat long and contemplated that. He'd come upon the tower by chance. And finding me trapped here, he'd felt compelled to act upon it. Some men did answer the call of chivalry, though, admittedly, none I knew of Lady Margaret's acquaintance.

Prince Kenzie had returned once, thinking to free me by using the rope. But it would not be so easy as that, and when he got clean away and out from under the impetus of his conscience, he must see how dangerous any further attempts could prove.

What importance had one girl, shut away in a prison room, to him? He, the youngest son of a king, had everything for which to live, a comfortable life, his health and freedom. He even had a young woman, also of high estate, waiting to wed him.

I wondered long why he'd felt it necessary to tell me that piece of information and why he'd followed it with a kiss—the first I'd ever received. The memory of that kiss still had the power to warm me clear through.

The point was, he would be mad to act against Lady Margaret and possibly embroil his father. If she found out, it would involve his family and all his kingdom in a dangerous dispute. Lady Margaret made a bad enemy for anyone.

Once away, he would see the truth of that. He must. Yet, as well I knew, the truth was hard to see, and hid well behind illusion. A gallant young man might well resist abandoning a woman he considered unfairly imprisoned. I hoped not, for his sake.

I hoped so, for mine.

I did not sleep that night. I did not even try. I left the shutters open through the dark hours and listened for any sounds of approach. Fear and superstition had me convinced Lady Margaret would come—that she would know about Kenzie's visit. That she would make me pay for it.

I watched dawn break over the forest. The breath froze in my lungs when I thought what this day might bring. It brought—

Nothing.

Nor did the next. Even though I supplied my near-raving mind with reasons why Kenzie might be delayed, the hope I'd sought to deny tormented me. I had no concept of the distance he needed to travel to reach home, and then to return. He and his men might hunt here, yes. In the heat of the chase, they had no doubt crossed onto Lady Margaret's lands. Far, indeed, from any village at the center of his father's kingdom.

Also, he meant to consult with the fellow, Justin, well versed in magic. That might well take time.

If he did not come, how could I return to my dismal, lonely existence?

For three days and four nights, nothing happened, beyond my intense fretting. The birds sang to me, if I not to them. Weather came and went.

My food and water continued to replenish, though I consumed little.

Kenzie MacAlver might well have been a dream.

I tell you, it near broke me. Even though I'd sought by any means I might to prepare myself for his abandonment, the reality of it looked to steal the last of my endurance.

The next day, around noon, I heard a disturbance. The birds flew up and from afar off came the sound of someone or something moving through the trees.

I hurried to the window and looked out, my heart beating up in my throat. A gray day it was, promising rain, though it did not rain just yet.

My breath suspended when I saw him stride out into the clearing, and my heart gave a great bound of mingled joy and disbelief.

Oh, heavens, oh, sweet mercy, he had come!

The rebound from despair near set me to raving again. I leaned dangerously far out over the casement, and drank in his appearance—brown hair gleaming, vitality fair radiating from him.

An entirely new emotion, one I could not name, blossomed and took hold of me. Satisfaction? Nay, not even that could describe it.

Swiftly, he approached the tower and called up to me. "RapAnn, RapAnn, let down your hair."

I did, performing the task with trembling hands. And, in so doing, I surrendered some of my disbelief. By letting down my hair, I opened myself to Kenzie and whatever he might bring, of good or ill.

He climbed up as he had before, a thousand emotions burgeoning in his eyes. I saw gladness and grief, resolve and stark courage, and I wondered what all that meant for me.

"RapAnn?" He laid his hands on mine, warm and vital. Once more, his presence dwarfed the chamber. "I am sorry I was awa' so long. It took time to consult with Justin and try to find a solution to your imprisonment."

Try to find a solution. Did that mean he had failed?

A thousand things I wanted to say. I longed to weep out my relief at seeing him, to tell him nothing else mattered. Only, it did matter.

"And—and had this Master Justin an answer for us?"

Reluctantly, he shook his head. "He is well-acquainted with the lady in question, and all her powers. The Witch of the Marches, she is called. And he studied on it every way he could. If she has placed an enchantment here, he does no' think it can be lifted. At least, he knows of no way."

I drew my hands from Kenzie's. "Then you should not have returned."

"Why do you say so, RapAnn?"

"You risk yourself for no good reason, and open yourself to terrible consequences. If she discovers you here, she will strike back, possibly even against your father's kingdom."

He drew himself up indignantly. "And am I to leave you here, then? Forget about you? Is that what you expect?"

"Yes. Do not mistake me. It is a fine and chivalrous impulse that has brought you back. And I am glad, beyond measure, to see you. But," I waved a hand at the window, "you have a life out there, even as I have not. You have a father and brothers who care about you. You have a betrothed who awaits your marriage."

"And," he challenged, "if my heart lies here, instead? What am I to do then, RapAnn? Go awa' and try to live wi'out my heart?"

I shook my head wildly. "You barely know me."

"Aye, madness, is it no'? But it does not seem to matter. List to me, RapAnn—this is no mere visit. I mean to stay, if you will have me."

"What!"

"I have brought many things, some here in my pack and more still on my horse's saddle. I intend to unload my mount, Swifter, and send him home. 'Tis why I chose him—he knows his way and will go when bidden."

"Your family, your father—"

"Justin knows the truth, though he will not tell. I also informed my brother, Reagan, that I am off about a quest. They will no' expect me home for some time."

Once more he seized my hands and squeezed them tight. "I may no' be able to get ye awa' out of here, RapAnn. But neither will I leave ye here forsaken and alone."

****

No matter how I argued, I could not dissuade Kenzie from that position. I will admit I tried hard and long, describing Lady Margaret's tendency toward vengeance, and what might befall him if she discovered him here.

He remained singularly unmoved by my arguments and busied himself emptying out his pack, even while listening to me.

He had, indeed, brought many things. A wealth of food, including a pouch of tiny frosted cakes. A number of books and a small chess set. Even a new pair of slippers, as mine had worn right through.

I protested anew. "But what if Lady Margaret returns and sees these things here? There is nowhere to hide them. Even if she does not see you—"

"Nevertheless, lass, meanwhile you shall ha' all these comforts."

When he finished unloading the pack, he climbed down and went off into the forest, to fetch still more goods from his horse. I watched from above for long, agonizing moments until he appeared once more.

Once he had climbed back up the rope of my hair, I told him, "You should not have sent your horse back home."

He quirked an inquiring brow at me.

"How will you escape, if she comes?"

"I will no'."

"But you must!"

"I mean to stand wi' you, RapAnn. Fight her if I can."

"You cannot!" I nearly sobbed. "Have you heard nothing I have told you?"

"I heard."

"It is madness," I declared. "There is no other excuse for it."

"My heart is here," he said, and repeating what he had told me before, took my shoulders between his hands. "Would you ha' me go awa' and try to live without my heart?"

"Yes." I began to weep. "Yes!"

"I canna'. I will no'."

Anger and fear seized me in equal measures. Always before had my fear of Lady Margaret centered on my own welfare. This—this felt much worse.

I declared, "I do not want you here."

He shook his head. "I am that sorry, RapAnn. I do no' believe you."

"There will be a price." I wept. "A terrible high price for this. There always is."

"Then, bonny lass, I will pay it without shirking."

Chapter Fourteen

Kenzie had brought not one but three blankets, along with a quantity of food, much of it preserved, in the second pack. He also informed me he should be able to climb down and hunt for us, as he'd brought a bow and arrows. I feared the replenishment of the food on which I'd been living would not keep up with double consumption. He bade me over and over not to concern myself with it.

Wrapped in one of the blankets, and well-protected, he'd brought another gift for me.

"You ken," he said as he unwrapped it, "I had no' much time to choose. I wished to get awa' back to you as quick as ever I could. But it came to me, how much time ye do spend combing out your hair."

He flipped back a fold of the blanket to reveal a silver-backed set of comb, brush, and hand mirror. Lovely the pieces were, all worked over in a design of tiny flowers with deep blue inlay—a far cry from my poor comb.

"Beautiful," I breathed.

Earnestly he told me, "You have lived on so little, so long. I wanted you to have something to enjoy. My sister did advise me. I did no' tell her for whom 'twas meant. I daresay she thought for Anastacia."

Anastacia—his betrothed. A beautiful name for a no doubt beautiful woman.

I reached out slowly and picked up the mirror. The handle felt cold to my touch. It lay face down, and I hesitated to turn it over.

"I have never seen myself," I told Kenzie.

"Eh?"

"Lady Margaret would not permit it. There were no mirrors or other polished surfaces. When she showed me off before her guests, and in the ballroom, even the windows would be covered. And when I went to her parlor to visit with Master Cole, there was no mirror."

"Only imagine," Kenzie said. "Most girls of my acquaintance spend a wealth o' time admiring their reflections."

"I have never seen mine," I repeated, and lifted my eyes to his face. "I am afraid to look, now."

"Do no' be, RapAnn." He closed his fingers over mine on the handle and lifted the glass. "You are gey beautiful."

Yes, but what is beauty? Can one's face possibly be beautiful if one has never seen it? Can one be other than beautiful to someone who cannot see at all?

Mirrors contain strong magic—so I must think Lady Margaret believed. Why else would she keep them from me while holding me prisoner? Did she think I might escape through one? Break the spell of her power?

I did not want to look. But Kenzie lifted the glass, and my hand with it, and turned the shining surface toward me.

I saw—

A girl, a stranger. She had a smooth white brow, two rounded cheeks slightly flushed, and a straight, narrow nose. Brows like two golden wings flew above large, blue eyes, set wide and fringed with dark gold lashes. More gold framed her face, ripples of long hair, the only part of her I recognized.

"That—that is me? It cannot be."

He tilted the glass slightly and part of his face also came into view, his image beside that of the girl. Through the magic of the mirror, he was reversed—his eyebrow with a slight quirk to it on the opposite side; a mole on his jaw leaped clear across.

Deep magic indeed.

"So it is, RapAnn. See me there beside you?"

"But it cannot be."

"Are you no' lovely, lass?"

"No." I pushed the glass away from me and turned on him. "How do I know that is truth? It is magical. It could be the merest illusion. I am who I am here..." I clasped a hand to my breast. "Inside."

He looked troubled. "RapAnn, I did not intend for my gift to upset you. Nor did I imagine you'd never seen yoursel'. Put it aside, if you ha' no liking for it."

I did so. Yet the thing had come into the room, and doubt had entered with it. Yes, the image of the girl in the mirror possessed beauty—not necessarily a good thing. In fact, it turned my stomach.

My appearance—presumably what I saw in the glass, if the mirror could be believed—accounted for the reason Master Cole desired me. Did it account also for the reason Kenzie had returned? Did he care not so much for me as for that image?

I would rather not be beautiful and, indeed, wished I were not. Which just goes to show you—be careful of that for which you wish.

****

Life with Kenzie seemed very full. Certainly, the tower room could barely contain his presence and his energy.

I had never lived with anyone, and I found it a leap doing so now. Do not misunderstand me—I wanted him to stay. I had spent so much time moored in loneliness and had craved a companion so long. But loneliness seemed my natural state, and we were thrown very closely together indeed.

Save for that first night, when we'd met, he left the narrow cot for me, and used two of the blankets to bed down on the floor beside it. Nothing untoward ever passed between us, save the clasping of hands and a good deal of laughter, yet it felt quite intimate.

The laughter seemed strange to me at first also, yet we laughed often, and I soon became accustomed. Kenzie possessed a lively mind and abundant energy. He enjoyed telling me stories about his home and family, far more fascinating than any I'd read in any book, and often quite amusing.

The first time I broke out laughing, at a tale of a tiny kitten that insisted on following his father the king everywhere and spoiled his dignity on a royal occasion, I startled myself. I could not remember ever having laughed so. Kenzie and I stared at each other for a moment before he laughed at my expression, and I joined him. We both laughed till our sides ached.

Perhaps I fell in love with his laughter—that deep, infectious chuckle, which just seemed to roll out of him. For fall in love I did, and swiftly. How could it be otherwise? The two of us, thrown together in such a way, combined with his kindness and gallantry in sharing my prison. How could I fail to fall head over heels for such a man?

Indeed, I'd thought myself taken with Antony, but that had been mere infatuation. Despite the differences in our origins and upbringings—wide indeed—Kenzie and I suited one another like two halves of the same story, being put together and suddenly making sense.

His energy completed my quietude, and my thoughtfulness balanced his tendency toward rashness. He remarked many times that he appreciated how I listened, and declared that, as the youngest son of a large family, no one ever heeded him so.

His generosity and good humor felt like a gift, and came in a package I could not resist. Yes, I loved him.

I did not think he returned my feelings, even though he stayed. And stayed... What kept him there in that prison with me, I could not say. His sense of chivalry, perhaps, taught to him and learned like a sacred edict, back in his father's kingdom.

For whatever reason, stay he did. Day spun into night and into day over and over again. Summer evolved into autumn, and Kenzie, with his bright, warm spirit, remained with me.

He might have left at any time, could have climbed back down the rope of my hair and hiked his way out through the forest. He did climb down from time to time, to go hunting or to stretch his legs—even to clean out the bottom of the garderobe. And when he finished, he always called up to me.

"RapAnn, RapAnn, let down your hair."

He could leave. I could not. And so, he stayed.

We passed the time with endless games of chess and another game he invented, with sticks and pebbles collected from the ground, which he called Cobble. I played for him on the small lute which he had, as promised, brought for me. And I sang. On rainy days—more frequent with the approach of autumn—we would lie with the shutters pinned closed, I on my cot and he stretched out on his blankets, and take turns telling stories.

His stories were true and mine, since I'd seen so little of the world, were fabrications. But I will tell you this, something I have learned: it was very difficult to tell the difference.

One afternoon when we did just that, while rain beat against the shutters and the room lay steeped in gloom, I bade him tell me about Anastacia.

He made an abrupt movement, as if startled or disturbed. "Must I?"

"You've told me about everyone else. Your brothers and sisters, your friends and your father, the king." Oh, how they must miss him! The way one might miss sunshine, for he surely lit my days. And what a ruler his father must be, bluff and kind, wise and forgiving.

Much like his son.

"I do no' wish to speak of Anastacia. I do no' even want to think about her. Especially while I am wi' you."

I said nothing. He had announced his betrothal to her as a reason he and I could never be more than we were now to one another. She must mean something to him.

"I barely know her," he admitted after the silence stretched long. "That is, I have met her a few times, and we ha' been betrothed since we were perhaps three or four years old. Arranged, as I say. Most marriages among royal families are arranged so."

Not that different from me, then. He might run free for a time, but when the moment came, his leash would be hauled in, and he would be afforded no choice.

"Folk envy a king's children," he mused. "And aye, we have many advantages. Plenty of food to eat, a good education, horses to ride, and hawks to follow. But there is a price to pay for it. I've spent the last score o' years refusing to think about Anastacia, or our promised marriage."

"A score of years?" I repeated. "Why are you not already wed?"

"Ha! I ha' escaped it so far, by the skin o' my teeth. Being the youngest son, tradition dictates the others should get wed ahead o' me. But," his voice dropped, "the day will come."

"When?"

"Within the next year, I do no' doubt."

I shivered where I lay, as if a cold wind blew through me. I would lose him. I could not bear the thought.

"What is she like, this woman who will be your wife?"

"I tell you, I scarcely know."

"Is she fair in face and form?" A standard taught to me at Lady Margaret's knee.

"Ah—she is no' ill to look upon. She has no' one whit o' your beauty."

I said, "Beauty is but the skin of the apple. All sweetness lies within."

"Then, RapAnn, why did you ask?"

Why had I? Something inside me just wanted to know. Was I jealous of a girl whom I'd never met? But that would make me small and spiteful; it would make me like Lady Margaret. The last thing I wanted to be.

I forced myself to say, "I wish you joy together."

"There will be no joy, RapAnn. None to be found." He sat up beside my cot. "For she might be lovely, indeed, and good natured and all the things 'tis declared a woman should be. She is no' you."

I sat up also. He grasped my hands and gazed into my eyes.

"Surely, lass, you maun know how I feel for ye?"

"I fear—I fear you have fallen under a spell, perhaps of my beauty. That is mere illusion, though, nothing of substance."

"I do no' stay for your face, bonny as it may be, or your form, RapAnn. Ha' I asked anything o' ye?"

"No."

"I maun wed with Anastacia, aye, because a promise has been given and I canna see my way out of it. But I've also promised to break the enchantment and see you free o' your prison. That I will do. Until I can, I will stay wi' ye, and I hope that proves to you what lies in my heart."

Chapter Fifteen

Following that conversation, our relationship changed in a way both subtle and profound. A shift occurred, and even if Kenzie did not speak of his feelings again, at least not aloud, the awareness had come to life between us and would not be hidden.

It troubled me. Let it be said with honesty here, most emotions—and especially those connected to relationships—bothered me. I suppose it could not be otherwise. I'd been forced to watch my family from afar and never experienced their affection. I'd known only Lady Margaret's twisted care, and been offered only Master Cole's unwanted attentions. I'd never had a friend.

Until now. For, above all the other things Kenzie became to me, he was first a friend. He laughed and played games with me, amused me and put up patiently with my foibles. He had put himself in danger and most loyally risked much for my sake.

I did, indeed, feel attracted to him. What maid would not? With his strong form, thick brown hair, and dancing brown eyes, he fitted my every notion of perfection. Yet I distrusted such attraction, just as I feared and distrusted the mirror now hidden at the bottom of a pile of clothing. What I saw in it had cost me Antony and caught Jeremiah Cole's interest. It had resulted in my imprisonment.

I suppose the best proof of my feelings for Kenzie lay in the fact that, henceforth, I worried for him. A cold fear crept over me that Lady Margaret would arrive and catch him there, which could only be the worse for both of us.

You must understand: the last thing I wanted was for him to leave. The very idea filled my mind with black devastation. But no—perhaps I wanted one thing less than that.

For harm to fall upon him.

As everything else, I broached the subject. A cool, breezy afternoon it was, so much a day of autumn that leaves fell from my surrounding trees like rain, bright gold and russet brown.

I'd been sitting at the window. I did not sing so much these days, though I did play the lute often for Kenzie's enjoyment. My songs, however, had already called to me what I needed.

All I needed.

Is need love? Is love a need? For the sake of it, can one give up everything else? A tangle with no beginning and no end.

Kenzie came and sat down beside me in that way he had—full of banked energy. I do not know how he disciplined himself to that tiny room, but he did.

He followed my gaze out the window before he switched it to my face. "Do ye wish to speak o' it?"

I turned my eyes on him in surprise. "Eh? Of what?"

"Whatever it is that troubles you."

"Why should you think—"

He laughed softly. "Lass, do you no' think I know ye well enough now to feel what you are feeling?"

My heart began to pound. "It is autumn. I do not know what has kept Lady Margaret away so long." I'd felt sure she would come before the autumn equinox. But so far, we'd been spared.

"Mayhap she's forgotten about ye."

"Nay, Kenzie. It's as we said before—if she'd forgotten me, the magic would stop. The food would cease replenishing itself."

"Perhaps she no longer cares."

"You know her not, if you can say so. She will be drawing out the punishment, fostering dread. Seeking still to break me."

I could not break, with him here. For he supplied my warmth, my mirth, my very strength.

With him gone? Oh, I feared I would shatter. Yet to just that end must I persuade him.

"Besides," I said, "it's as if I can feel her these past few days, focused upon me. I think she comes soon."

He took my hand in his. As always at his touch, comfort flooded me, but this time not enough.

"That is but your dread talking, lass. You merely fear she will come soon."

I shook my head and clutched his fingers in turn. "You must leave me, Kenzie."

"Ha!" He stared at me with outraged eyes. "I will no'."

"Listen to me. Winter fast approaches. You do not want to be here then."

He glanced outside as if trying to imagine the scene covered in snow, nothing between my living space and the cold save a pair of shutters. "If you think I will agree to abandon you—"

"Kenzie." I drew him closer to me, tugging on his

hands. "You do not want her to find you here. You do *not*."

"RapAnn—"

"Her anger is a terrible thing, so cold it burns. There is no telling what she would do to you. You do not want to find out." I did not want to find out. I could not endure it.

"Sweet lass. 'Tis kind in you to worry for me. But even should she catch me here—which she will no'— what can she do? I am a prince, the son of a powerful king. She will no' dare cross him."

"She will. She is used to taking people's lives into her hands and trifling with them. I do not believe any, even your father, can stand against her."

"No one is that powerful."

"You say that only because you've not lived beneath her rule. I have—all my life."

"Aye, and so you can see naught else."

"Still, I think you should go, for a time." It cost me to say those words. It cost me dear. "Go home to your people for the winter. They will be worrying for you."

"You suppose I will walk awa' and let you face what may come, alone? Is that what ye think o' me, lass?"

"I think your honest heart and sense of chivalry may cost too much. I am used to being on my own. I will do well enough."

But I lied. I no longer felt sure I could live through a winter here, without him. My world had altered. He had brought something from beyond the tower's confines. Bleak, indeed, to lose it all.

Kenzie gazed once more into my eyes. What he saw there softened his gaze.

"RapAnn, it touches me to the heart that ye should hold such concern for me. Know this—if Lady Margaret comes wi' her guards, as ye ha' described, we will hear her from afar. I will ha' time then to climb down and awa'."

"And what of all these things? The extra clothing you brought me, our games—this lute? She will know when she sees them, Kenzie, if not before."

"Hush, lass. We will ha' time to gather up all the trappings. I will tak' them wi' me, into the forest."

"And if we do not hear her in time?" The fear clawing at my belly colored my voice. "Best to leave now. Take these things with you." All my comforts. But, nay—for he was that. "You can return later, if you will. Once you are certain she has gone."

"RapAnn, RapAnn, I am no' certain I can bring mysel' to leave you at all."

"You must."

"Let me stand and face her wi' you."

Ah, and there spoke the king's son. He believed, still, in justice. In right. But what happened to right, to light, with the coming of darkness?

"If you stand against her," I said with absolute certainty, "you will fall." And I knew to the core of my being his pain—witnessed—would be far worse than my own.

****

My fears proved justified, after all. On a cold, windy afternoon that spit rain, more than half turned to snow, we were very nearly caught out.

Kenzie had closed the shutters against the sleet, and I sat playing softly on my lute, by the dim light of the fire. He lay on his blankets, more than half asleep, I do not doubt, when beneath the rattle of the shutters, my ears caught a sound.

I stopped playing and lifted my head. "What is that?"

"Um?" I'd been right; he sounded drowsy.

"Kenzie—" Cold drenched me from the head downward. I set the lute aside. "Kenzie, arise. Arise! She comes."

He leaped to his feet all in one movement, it seemed, and stared at me. We both hurried to the window. He clawed the shutters open.

I heard it clearly then, even over the wind. The jingle of harness. The sound of hoofbeats, half muffled on damp ground.

Raw panic gripped me by the throat. "Go! You must go now. Gather up what you brought. Swiftly!"

I dashed about the room, snatching up one of the sacks in which he'd transported my niceties so long ago. Into it went the clothing—fortunately I wore one of my original dresses—the chess set, the beloved lute. I even shucked the pretty slippers from my feet and tossed them in. His blankets, his cloak—which I flung about his shoulders with unsteady hands.

All the while, he stood and stared at me rebelliously. "Lass—I will no' abandon ye."

"You must. You must! Oh, quickly."

"I am no' afraid o' her—"

"I am. I am! Oh, Kenzie, please." I acted as never before, seized his face between my hands and kissed him. "Go, for my sake."

Whatever he saw in my eyes convinced him. He tossed the sacks, now filled, from the window even as I fastened my hair to the hook.

Half way out the opening, he paused to kiss me again.

"I'll return to you, darling girl. I do so promise."

In a frenzy, I cried, "Go!"

I watched him climb down the rope of my hair and land lightly on the ground. He gathered up the sacks and cast one lingering glance up at me.

Go, my heart cried. And he did.

Chapter Sixteen

"RapAnn, let down your hair!"

The cry came up to my ears like the clang of a bell, one that pealed doom. I felt ill, hot and cold by turns, and I trembled where I stood, my fingers clamped hard on the casement.

Kenzie had barely made it away around the tower and, presumably into the forest—for I could not see, I could not see!—before the birds flew up from the trees, and a party of three entered the clearing.

As before, Lady Margaret came at the head of two guards.

Over and over again, my eyes searched the ground, terrified Kenzie might have dropped something—just one item would give me away. I saw nothing.

Even more than that, I feared Kenzie's sense of gallantry would cause him to return, face off against the guards, and try to win my freedom.

I believed, to my very toes, if he tried he would not succeed. He would, instead, pay for the privilege.

I would pay any price rather than see that happen. For at that moment, having watched him climb down and hie away—having lost him—I knew in full how I loved him. More than that, I knew for the first time there might be something worse, in this world, than facing Lady Margaret's cold wrath.

Watching Kenzie face it.

Funny, how the absence of someone can prove his value. Funny too, that love can make you feel so strange, weak and yet strong at the same instant, like you could collapse, like you could fight to the death.

I'd resented Lady Margaret in the past. God knew, I'd held out against her. But I'd never battled. That, for Kenzie's sake, I now felt willing to do.

Go, I told him again in my mind. *Go far.* This I said, even as I watched Lady Margaret pause below the tower and look up at me.

Surprisingly for all that had happened, she looked the same. Haughty, powerful, and so very confident.

Her eyes flashed as she called again, "RapAnn, let down your hair!"

What if I refused? She would get in by magic, the same as when first she brought me to this prison. I could never forget that, even before a cold and heartless woman, she was a witch.

She would have her way. Did that fact not lie at the very root of this contest between us?

At that moment, it seemed so inevitable. The strength lent by Kenzie's presence left me swiftly in the face of Lady Margaret's power.

But perhaps I did not lose all my strength. If I could stall her, Kenzie would have time to get clean away. I had to act as if I'd been languishing here, as if nothing had changed, even though everything—everything had.

Taking my time with it, I slung my hair over the hook and let it down.

It had grown much, over the course of the summer. It now pooled about my feet in a river of gold, if I left it unplaited, which I rarely did.

She climbed up it the way a spider does a web, all knees and elbows. I swear I could feel the evil of her, like an approaching cloud, a miasma.

She came over the sill, and I unhooked my hair and turned to face her.

"Well, girl?" Her cold, gray eyes snapped as she swept me with a look, up and down again. "I confess, I half-expected to find you dead after so long."

So she hadn't been able to feel me from afar? Consternation hit me at that. Had I been ascribing to her greater powers than she possessed?

Yet my voice quivered when I replied, "D-did you, my lady?"

It made her smile. She waved a hand. "Perished from boredom, perhaps. Or I thought you might have dashed yourself from the tower after all."

"No, my lady." I lowered my eyes, hoping she would not see the memories that lay there—long, sunny afternoons filled with laughter, and nights with steady companionship.

Oh, my love, my heart cried. *Flee, and quickly.*

"No. Did you wonder why I kept away so long?"

"Yes, my lady."

"There have been developments at the manor. I come now to advise you of them."

My thoughts leaped. What could have occurred? What, that would affect me?

Had she come to set me free? I raised my eyes again, trying to read her intentions.

I had ached for freedom, so long. For the first part of my imprisonment here, it had obsessed my mind— the ways and means of escape. That, though, had been before Kenzie entered my life. If she took me away out

119

of here and back to her manor, I might never see him again.

That thought felt like a hard blow to the gut. I began to tremble anew.

"What—what developments, my lady?"

Her smile sharpened. She liked the meekness of the question, and that I'd lost what she no doubt termed my defiance. She enjoyed wielding her power.

"Master Cole has grown weary of waiting for you to come to your senses, and has lost interest. In fact, he has found another plaything. She was presented to him at the autumn equinox fete."

"Oh!" Ill news for the unknown young woman, but might it be good for me? It must be.

"So you see," Lady Margaret waved a finger at me, chiding, "you have spoiled things for yourself, as well as earning my lasting disfavor by spurning my dear friend."

I barely heard those words. Dared I ask for my release—a life of my own somewhere out in the world?

But she would never grant that to me, not if she believed it was what I wanted. I must be clever—far more so than ever before.

"My lady, I am not worthy of a place in your household."

"Eh?" Her eyes narrowed. "What is this you say?"

"I have had long to think, during my time here— nothing to do but think—and realize I have been woefully defiant and undeserving of all you have given me over the years."

She made a sharp sound almost like a "Ha!" and her voice grew several degrees colder when she said, "You have caused me a great deal of trouble, and no mistake. I swore to myself I would break you. Tell me, RapAnn, have I succeeded?"

"My lady, you have."

I could not tell if she believed me. She took a turn around the tiny room, as if her doubt made her restless. "Be that as it may, what am I to do with you now? Master Cole says he no longer wants you, and you are certainly suited to no other purpose."

"I am no use to you." None, other than a captured mouse might be, to a sated cat. Did she enjoy tormenting me? Exercising the sharpness of her cruelty?

"I suppose there is little to be done save take you home with me. Yet—"

She paused suddenly in her pacing, precisely as if she'd caught sight of—or scented—something that captured her attention. I went rigid with alarm. What had she seen? Had Kenzie forgotten an item? One of the chess men, perhaps, or even a stray pebble from Cobble. There could be no object in this room that Lady Margaret had not brought, or she would know someone else had been here.

"What is that?"

She faced the corner, where lay my other two dresses, neatly folded. I could see nothing else on the floor, nothing—

But the tip of a silver handle sticking out from beneath a fold of the blue cloth.

I went hot and cold with horror, all the way to my soul. Oh, no, oh, no—I'd forgotten the mirror. I'd tucked it away so long ago, hidden it because I feared its magic and the image it could show to me.

Perhaps, from the first, I'd feared this very

moment. But I'd forgotten, forgotten to guard against it, at the end.

Her voice rose as she repeated, "What is that?"

I did not speak. I could not. I wanted to fall through the stone floor, to disappear, to turn to ash and blow away.

She stepped forward and plucked the hand mirror from beneath the fabric, holding it between thumb and forefinger as if it might scald her.

She turned accusing eyes on me. "Where did you get this?"

God help me, I could think of nothing to say, no excuse that made any sense. I bit my lip until it bled.

Her voice became a shriek. "Answer me, stupid girl!"

She struck me with her other hand, the one not holding the mirror. The blow took me off my feet and up against the wall beside the window. Once I fell, she turned the full power of her gaze on me. I'd seen her angry before. Everyone in the manor feared her anger. But I'd never beheld aught to match the rage that now looked at me from her eyes.

She'd gone white with it, and two flags of color flew in her cheeks. Her eyes—but I have no words to describe them.

At that moment, I believed I would die. I wondered if I'd do better to fling myself out the window. Better crushed below than suffering the fate she would deal out to me.

I scrambled up and onto the sill of the casement.

She hauled me back, fingers on the fabric of my dress. Her nails, sharp as daggers, bit through the cloth and scored my flesh.

"Get back here," she shrieked. "Answer me!"

The birds flew up again at that shriek. The very trees seemed to shudder.

Lady Margaret tossed me down, struck me again, and waved the mirror in my face. "How did you get your hands on this?"

I covered my head with my arms. I am not proud of such cowardice, but it occurred. I waited for the next blow or more likely a kick, since I sprawled ready to her feet.

I wondered how long it would take me to die, how many blows.

But she did not touch me. Instead she lifted the mirror and closed her eyes, pressing it to her forehead.

I swear, I felt the magic come. It fell dark and noisome, like the wave of dread that creeps over a soul in the wee hours of the night.

She stiffened and hissed. Her eyes came open, and in them I saw—

Rage and knowing, a terrible power.

"A man brought this here," she announced, certain as death. "Who is he?"

Chapter Seventeen

"No," I said. The word came readily to my lips. I'd spent so much time in the past delivering it to her, it had become a learned response. But even as I spoke, I knew how futile was the denial.

She would not believe me. I was lost. My one hope lay in sparing my love.

"A peddler," I said desperately, even as her gaze bored into me. It felt like cold steel penetrating my mind. "He happened by and left that for me."

"Liar!" She sneered, "Peddlers do not give away their wares. You have had a man here. I can smell him on this." She waved the mirror. "In the very air, now that I think on it."

Her eyes narrowed. "You have had some fellow in here. You let down your hair for him, did you not? Of course you did—it is the only way he could get in. What else did you give him? What did you trade for this pretty trinket? Your virtue?"

"No. No!"

"Tell me the truth, or I swear you will regret it."

So strong was her will, I almost told. Very nearly did it come spilling from me. If I spoke of Kenzie, though, she would go after him. And not even her will, her anger, could make me betray him.

"Was it that accursed musician? Did he find you?"

"No." As soon as the word left my lips, I knew I

should have said yes, instead, should have thrown Antony to the wolves.

"And this!" She waved the mirror so wildly, I thought she meant to strike me with it. "A glass, of all things. So you wished to see yourself, did you? To admire your beauty? Well, girl, what did you think?"

"I wish I'd never seen myself." To be sure, I wished I'd never seen, or touched, the mirror.

"Did you admire your beauty, RapAnn?"

"No. No, I wish I were not beautiful."

Something ignited in her eyes, twin flames. "You suppose I believe that? All women wish to be beautiful. 'Tis the one power they possess."

She was wrong—that I knew to my soul. The one power I'd ever possessed lay in a spirit that would not break. But how could I, shut away all my life, possibly know better than she, with all her wisdom?

"Here—let us look. Let us admire." She dragged me up by the hair. So terrified was I, I barely registered the pain.

She bent down next to me, all coiled power, and turned the glass as Kenzie once had, so it reflected us together. And oh! What I saw.

I have said Lady Margaret was beautiful, in a proud, haughty way, with her smooth skin and black-streaked auburn hair. But in the glass, I saw something else—her face bore haggard lines and her skin looked dry as paper. Rage possessed every feature.

Beside that face, mine looked fresh as a flower. But I feared the terror in the wide, blue eyes.

"Lovely, aren't you?" she grated. "Is that what brought him here, your lover? Do you think he would still want you, if you were as hideous as you are disobedient?"

I did not know. God save me, I did not know.

She smiled at my reflection. "You think he will come back to you once I am gone, this mysterious stranger? Time for another lesson, RapAnn—one you will never forget."

She waved her fingers, like a spider wiggles its legs to spin a thread. I felt the magic before I saw its reflection in the glass, and I tried to pull away. Desperation allowed me to break free of her, but I could not move far.

Not far enough.

When the spell hit me, it brought pain. It seared my skin the way acid might, burning beneath the surface. I cried out and covered my head again.

"Be careful what you wish for, girl."

What had she done to me?

She stepped past me to the window. There, she hauled me up, will-he, nil-he, and ordered, "Let down your hair, you wretch."

Still suffused with pain, I obeyed, my hands trembling violently. When the rope hung ready, she looked at me and smiled in satisfaction.

"You have what you deserve, RapAnn. I shall leave you this, eh? So you may continue to admire yourself."

She tossed the mirror at my feet before going over the sill with agility that defied her years.

I unwound my hair from the hook and, like one struck, watched her and the two guards stride away. Oh, how aware I was of that glass lying at my feet! I wanted with all my being to pick it up and look. I feared with all my being to do so. I did not move.

The pain in my face slowly died. By the time the last hoof-fall faded from hearing, I felt only a faint burning sensation.

I went into the garderobe and vomited, over and over again. I retched until I thought my stomach would come up through my throat. Then I crept like some deformed insect back to the window, where the mirror lay face down.

A thousand thoughts tumbled through my mind. At least Kenzie remained safe. At least she had not taken me back to the manor with her. But I was still a prisoner here.

And she had done something terrible to me.

I picked up the glass and dragged it, still face down, into my lap where I sat beneath the window. I sat that way until the light began to fade and the forest grew as silent as a tomb. And I realized if I didn't look now, I would not be able to see the damage until morning. A whole night, not knowing.

I raised the glass and looked.

****

How many tears can a woman weep? I found out, that night.

I'd never been a vain girl. Heaven knew, until I first looked into the glass, I'd had no cause for vanity. And even then, I'd feared what I saw, as if something in me knew it would eventually come back upon me.

I had lost so much already, in my life. The love of a family, contact with the outside world. The right to choose my fate. My freedom and Kenzie's company.

Now, though, I'd lost even what I did not wish to possess.

I struggled to understand why it affected me so

deeply. I'd never wished to be beautiful. But she had done this to me—done it out of cruelty—and left me to stew in it. What answer could there be but tears?

I wept and, utterly exhausted, dozed and woke to weep again. I tossed the mirror from the window at first light, and watched it shatter on the ground. Seven years bad luck, I thought miserably, and laughed like a madwoman.

At least with the mirror shattered, I would not have to look at myself again. I had no need to. The image had become seared onto the insides of my eyelids. Cheeks that had once been round, now withered and pocked by scars. Nose, askew. Eyebrows scruffy and marked by scabs. The eyes that had been set so wide and looked so clear, squinted and faded to the palest blue, lashes all but gone.

I waited, that day, for Lady Margaret to return, to either finish the job and kill me or relent and restore my appearance. But of course I should have known she would never relent. What further intentions she had for me, I could not guess. Master Cole certainly would not want me now, even if he tired of his new plaything. She might well leave me to die.

Yet the water kept flowing in the enchanted pitcher, which I used in a frantic effort to wash away the blight that now beset me. The food, which I did not touch—I could not—remained fresh.

She did not come back. Nor did Kenzie. About him, I dared not think. I wanted and needed him, longed for him, but I could not bear the prospect of him seeing me so changed.

By nightfall, I had considered dashing myself from the tower window and ending my predicament. Would I die instantly? Would I lie there, broken, for days on end until the elements finished me? Did it matter? Lying there, sooner or later I would perish. If Kenzie could no longer love me, I reasoned, I had nothing for which to live.

I had lost all.

****

Come dawn, the agony of my emotions had abated to a dull, if constant, ache. Rain moved in over the forest and all the birds—those that hadn't already flown away to the south—took to their nests and fell silent. I heard only falling rain.

Did the world weep for me? I could not be so conceited as to think so. The world cared naught for one scrap of humanity. It never had.

Trapped in my tower, I paced until spent. I drank water, only to throw it up again in the garderobe. As I paced, I prayed.

I prayed Kenzie would not return. For what could I say to him, if he did? What excuse could I make when he bade me let down my hair for him and give him admittance?

Into my life.

Into my world.

Into my heart.

Should I gaze into his warm brown eyes and watch the admiration there die? Watch the love die, the only love I'd ever known?

But he did not return, even though time passed—days following nights. I began to worry that she had hunted him down, that she knew somehow—via her magic—who he was. That she'd scoured the forest after she left me and found him still journeying afoot.

That, rather than my ruination, was the worst thing I could imagine.

Chapter Eighteen

New life, like new hope, does not grow in autumn. It is a time for dying back, for shutting down and sleeping. From my windows at the manor, I used to watch Lady Margaret's gardeners put her formal garden to bed. They would prune down the plants that needed it, cover the delicate ones, and harvest great bushes of herbs. Nothing grew, until spring.

But now, new life began to spring up all around the tower.

I noticed it first about a week after that day—that dreadful day—when Lady Margaret changed me. Bright bits of green sprouted, filling the area between the forest and the trees.

It looked so strange. Most of the trees had now been stripped bare by rain and wind. In all my time at the tower, the area between those trees and the walls that enclosed me had remained clear. Now something grew, and at an unnatural rate.

I could not, of course, see all the way around the tower. But I imagined the tiny green plants surrounding me.

Left by Lady Margaret's magic? I suspected so, but why? What need had she to further beleaguer me?

For days, I watched them grow with disconcerting speed. Tiny buds one day, strong stems the next, and very soon gangly seedlings. Very green they were, the color of the apple Kenzie had once given me. Ripe with life.

I fancied I understood it then. Lady Margaret wished to enclose me in a cage of living vitality—me, whom she'd withered. Her cruelty simply knew no bounds.

Watching the sprouts grow gave me something upon which to focus. The year swiftly died, and there wasn't much light, but I swear those vines grew during the night and would be taller when I looked out each morning.

For it soon became evident that vines they were. As they grew, they twined and twisted together, forming a solid wall of dense greenery.

At last, I truly did understand. She'd fortified my prison, made it impenetrable. If Kenzie did return, he would never get through that tangle.

She did not comprehend that she did me a favor. I could not bear it if he returned, even though I wanted him more than anything else in the world.

****

The vines grew to a height of perhaps twelve feet—not high enough that I might use them to climb down from my prison. One would have had to be mad anyway, to try, for they sprouted long thorns, like spikes, as an added defense.

Despite their bright green color, which maintained even after the snow came and they were dusted with white, they gave off a bitter smell. That bitter tinge now filled and tainted my days. I am not too proud to say, faced with that vile wall of vines, I crumbled. A year had I spent in this prison. I'd been happier than I could have imagined here, and far more desperately unhappy. Now I faced another winter alone. Perhaps, at that point, I merely lost my strength, the inner certainty that had allowed me to stand against Lady Margaret when I possessed no other resources.

Funny to think my inner strength, which had naught to do with outer appearances, could be so affected by the loss of my beauty. I knew quite well that appearance equated illusion, just as strength equated truth. Perhaps, after all, I merely feared that if Kenzie saw me like this he would love me no longer, that it had been but my face he loved, and never me.

But he did not return.

I will spare you the tale of that winter, my second spent in the tower. It was grim, dark, and endless. I'd never been so lonely. One cannot miss, so they say, what one's never had. But I'd shared Kenzie's bright company, with its warmth and laughter, and felt the lack in full.

I missed him almost as much as I dreaded the possibility of his return.

But he never came. No one did. Not Lady Margaret, not a party of stray hunters, or even a rampant boar. All the birds had gone. Never had I felt more alone.

I slept much, that winter. I lay beneath the single blanket Kenzie had left me in place of the one he'd shredded—one touched by his hands—and tried to shut the world away. I ate little. I sang not at all.

Eventually spring came. The songs of the returning birds heralded it. They came in ones and twos and began their mating rituals, as old as time. The sun soon followed, crawling across my windowsill a bit earlier every morning and departing a bit later every day.

I lived on.

I did not know what to expect from that spring. At first, I thought Lady Margaret might return. Then it came to me, even she could not get through that defensive wall of green, save by magic.

Kenzie would not be able to reach me, even if he returned.

I tried to imagine where he might be. With his family, of whom he'd told me so much? Hunting with his brothers, teasing his sisters in that gentle way he had? Paying court to Anastacia?

Lying dead beneath a drift of brown leaves in the forest, if Lady Margaret had found him.

I will admit, some mornings I wept, despite the beauties of spring. Not knowing is a terrible cruelty. But the birds sang to me. They alone were able to fly above the tangle of green. The flash of color from their wings served to please me, as did the warm air coming in.

One day, I decided to comb out my hair, neglected all winter. It now pooled on the floor at my feet, my one remaining claim to beauty, for it alone had escaped Lady Margaret's dreadful spell. I sat and worked at removing the tangles, a lengthy task.

And as I combed my hair, I sang.

I sang for the first time since I'd lost everything.

At first, I'll admit, the song was just the ghost of a tune, a mournful one at that. A lament. But the birds flew closer to listen, and the comb moved in rhythm, easing my task. I sang on.

As it always had, the music served to comfort me. When the days grew longer, my voice became stronger. Alone there save for the birds, and with even the shards of the broken mirror hidden beneath the mat of green thorns, there were moments I forgot my appearance.

****

In the stories they tell of me, I am always beautiful. That beauty seems to convey all other virtues—I am also gentle and virtuous and patient despite my lengthy imprisonment.

But stories are not the same as truth. Even after all I'd suffered, I could not declare I recognized the truth. There is such a fine line between it and illusion, created by magic or the power of desire.

If no one laid eyes on me ever again, my face need not appear as I'd viewed it in the glass. And as spring flirted with summer, it seemed no one ever would see me again.

The bitter scent given off by the vines below the tower grew stronger as they ripened. And, they bloomed. Little, tight buds of red appeared all over the stems. At first, they looked like nothing so much as drops of blood. One by one they opened into small, dark roses. And the thorns on the vines turned black, as if they too became ripe.

When it rained, which happened little that season, the roses all turned their faces up to catch the water. And for days after, the moisture would trickle down in red, as if the flowers bled.

I found the sight distressing, and tried not to look. I combed out my hair and made new songs, some to ward off the ill magic of what lay below. Can one weave a spell from music?

Perhaps so.

I have said I slept much through that winter and into the spring, and in the summer also. Mercifully, when I slept I dreamed but rarely. On one particular afternoon, however, while the sun scribed its path overhead and the flowers emitted their drowsy, evil scent, I must have drifted off with my comb in my hand. And then I did dream. I dreamed I sang one of my sweetest songs.

"RapAnn, RapAnn, let down your hair!"

The call penetrated the groggy layers of sleep, or perhaps originated there. For no one had called up to me for so long.

Did I know that voice? Not Lady Margaret's, sharp and haughty, nor Kenzie's, rich and robust, though the sound had my eyes flying wide open, and my heart pounding up in my throat.

Panicked, I flew to the window. The sun had moved far to the west while I slept. Nothing else appeared different. I could see only green tangles splashed with red and the treetops beyond.

"RapAnn, are ye no' there?"

Ah, God! That did sound like Kenzie, his voice changed and weighted by pain. I nearly fell down where I stood, and had to grip the casement to stay upright.

"RapAnn, for the love o' God, let down your hair for me."

"Kenzie?" I whispered the name first, whispered it like a hope not even I could hear. I repeated it more loudly, seeking truth in the face of impossibility.

"Kenzie?"

"Aye, lass. I beg ye let me up."

A trick? It must be, for I could not imagine Kenzie begging for anything. I could not see who might stand below, not through the thick vines. It could be anyone—anything. A troll or some other magical being

136

sent by Lady Margaret to beleaguer me. Lady Margaret herself, with her voice disguised.

And if it truly were Kenzie? If he'd returned to me?

Oh, the doubt, fear, and longing that filled me at that possibility. Staggering joy that I might see him again.

Stark horror, that he might see me.

Both came crashing in upon me in near-equal measures. For he had loved me best in all the world. But—when he saw me so altered, would he love me still?

Could I bear to let down my hair, allow him to climb up and look me in the face? Could I stand and watch as the love in his eyes died?

You see, I'd never been certain why Kenzie loved me. I'd never believed. And truth, as I more than half suspected, lay only in belief.

How long I stood so, torn by indecision, I could not say. For the first time since I'd arrived at the tower, it felt less a prison than a protective fortress.

If I did not allow it, Kenzie could not come in. If he did not come in, he could not cease to love me.

For if I could not see him down among the vines, that meant he could not see me there in the casement.

Oh, what to do?

"RapAnn, for mercy's sake!"

Mercy. The smile in his eyes when he looked at me. His endless patience with my moods and fears. His willingness to share my prison in order to remain near me.

He had promised to return to me, and so he'd done. Could I reward such constancy by turning him away?

That one thought, above all others, had me gathering up the length of my hair and twisting it between my hands.

I called down to him, "Wait." I wound the hair around the hook and played out the great length of it between my palms, watching it snake down against the gray stones, keeping it there so it would not get caught up when it reached the vines.

"There," I called as it trailed down. "Against the tower!"

I caught just a glimpse of his hands as he reached forward. I felt the tug as he pulled on the rope of my hair. The iron hook took all the strain when he began to climb. My heart pounded, pounded, and the vines rustled and grasped at him as he came, keeping his body close to the tower in an effort to escape them. His head came into view, that smooth brown cap I recognized with yet another leap of the heart. And his hands, strong, square and tanned, sprinkled with what I took to be bright red rose petals.

I wanted to turn away before he came over the sill, to hide my face in a cloth or in my hair, so he would not see. But I remained pinioned there by the iron hook, and by my refusal to let him fall.

I will admit, I turned my eyes away, giving in to the foolish illusion that if I didn't see him, he wouldn't see me. So I did not watch him crawl over the stone sill.

I did not at once look into his face.

My first intimation that something was very much amiss came when he collapsed at my feet. His breath sounded harsh and ragged, surely more so than could be attributed to the climb. And when he spoke my name, "RapAnn," I heard what sounded like a sob in his throat.

"Kenzie?"

He lifted his face to me and I gasped in dismay. I sank to my knees beside him, a woman with no remaining strength.

Chapter Nineteen

"What has happened to you, Kenzie? Tell me what's happened? Oh, my love—"

I must have repeated those words a score of times. I spoke them through bitter lips as I gazed into his beloved face. I sobbed them as I realized what must have befallen him, as the horror of it came over me in waves.

He said only, "I returned to you. I promised I would."

"Yes. Yes, my love."

Unsure what to do, unable to fathom how to help him, I drew him to my bosom, dire injuries and all.

For those were not rose petals I'd seen on his hands, but drops of blood. Kenzie's blood. When I drew him into my arms, he clutched at me like a drowning man. For one glorious moment, it all returned to me, the comfort and the sense of belonging. But that could not last.

Very gently, I put him from me. "Oh, Kenzie—Kenzie, let me see. I must do something to help you."

But I did not know how I might treat such terrible injuries.

He must have fought his way through the vines to reach the tower, to reach me. But oh, he had paid a terrible price! For the thorns had caught at and torn him. His clothing, shredded. His hair full of the vicious, black things, that winked like jet. His hands and his face oozing blood. His eyes—

Oh, God, oh, sweet merciful God! His poor eyes!

I gasped and began to weep.

"Is it so terrible, RapAnn?" he asked. "Are the wounds so dire?"

"Kenzie, they are dire, indeed."

"I cannot see you. There is too much blood. It has blinded me."

So there was, a terrible amount of blood—a veritable welter of it seeping from his hands, covering the fabric of his tunic and streaking his face. It pooled in both eye sockets, or more accurately leaked from his torn eyes.

I could not see his dear eyes for blood. Just as he could not see me.

That realization caused another tangle of emotions. Horror remained predominant, distress for this man I loved—that you must believe. But a hint of relief also came to me. He could not see me, at least not yet.

"I am sure once we get the blood cleared away, you will." My voice shook. "Sit there. Let me fetch some water."

Did that water, which pooled in the ewer, possess magical properties? I'd always suspected so. Now I tore pieces from the hem of my dress and carried the ewer to Kenzie where he'd collapsed.

A thousand questions crowded my mind. But clearly Kenzie, my strong, brave hero, did not possess the ability to answer them yet.

"Just lie quietly," I bade him, "while I see you made right."

But I could not make him right. I worked over his

hurts, tending the worst of them before the lesser, until the light faded from the sky and the water in the ewer threatened to run out. I pulled countless black thorns from his clothing, only to discover they'd penetrated the flesh beneath. The thorns were as long as my palm and so wickedly sharp, I scratched myself any number of times just in handling them.

I could not stanch the blood. As soon as I wiped it away, it seeped forth again. It seemed as if the thorns must possess some property that made the wounds weep.

They had gouged furrows in Kenzie's cheeks. And as I saw in the brief moments when I wiped away the blood, they had indeed torn his eyes.

I wept the whole time I tended him. He had done this, faced the maze of green vines, for me—for me. How can I express what that meant? He had kept his promise, but at such a price.

At last, there at the base of the window, he slept. I tore up the last of my dress and, not knowing what else to do, bound a broad bandage over his eyes. Exhausted, I cuddled close to him and also fell asleep.

Oh, the evil dreams that beset me that night! Dreams of blood and pain. I dreamed Lady Margaret returned, all cold and angry. She removed the bandage from Kenzie's eyes and ordered him, "Look. Look at her!"

His expression of disgust when he beheld my face made me curl in upon myself, shrink away into a worthless ball—just what Lady Margaret always declared me.

Morning came, as it always does even at the worst of times. I awoke to the first light and the songs of the birds. Chilly air poured through the window, and the man in my arms felt cold.

Was he dead? No, but a change had taken place while we slept. The blood on his cheeks had dried and clotted. Though the bandage that covered his eyes was stained with blood, it had not soaked through.

I touched his chest and felt it rise and fall in shallow breaths. No, not dead, thank heaven. By a miracle, or an act of sheer will, he was here with me, and mine to look after, come what may.

I scrambled up, stiff as an old woman, and peered out the window. A breeze blew, stirring the vines which waved their flowers at me in an ugly parody of Kenzie's wounds. Over the trees, rain clouds gathered. A grim sight, indeed.

That, though, scarcely mattered. My love had returned to me—if he could love me still.

I brought the blanket from the cot and tucked it well around him. The water in the ewer had replenished during the night, but we would need to use it carefully, to have enough for two.

Should I tell him the truth? Before I stripped the bandage from his eyes and discovered if he could see, should I tell him what Lady Margaret had done to me? To be sure, I did not want to, but fairness demanded it. I had occupied Lady Margaret's reality all my days, and lived through many illusions. But I would not lie to this brave man.

After several moments, he stirred. I knelt back down beside him.

"Kenzie? How do you feel?"

"I canna' see you, RapAnn, lass."

"I know."

He raised both hands to the bandage and tugged at it.

"My darling, do you remember what happened to you?"

He stilled an instant. "What did ye call me?"

"My darling." For he was that. "My love." He was that, also. "The light of my life."

"Och, 'twas all worth it, then, RapAnn, worth anything, if ye care for me. I had to return to ye, and no' just because I promised. But 'twas a terrible, hard journey back. It took me so long." He reached out and clasped my hand. Our fingers twined together.

I would not weep—I would not weep again. No time for tears, now.

Slowly, Kenzie said, "I had to find ye—I could no' rest. 'Twas as if I'd left half o' myself here in this tower."

"Hush, now. You'd better drink some water. You took little enough last night. And then—and then we will remove that bandage and discover what you can see."

"Aye, but not just yet. First, I need this." He drew me into his arms, and held me tight. And yes, the embrace dampened the fear and quieted the panic fluttering in my gut. When Kenzie held me so, comfort enfolded me, and the world retreated beyond the stone walls of that room.

Prison and refuge, in one.

Outside, the clouds scudded in, and the birds quieted their songs. It started to rain.

I stirred then. "Come, we cannot stay here with the rain coming in."

I helped him up and led him to the cot. I persuaded

him to drink a cup of water, and after, with trembling hands, I unwound the bandage from his eyes.

"How bad is it, RapAnn?"

"Bad." I did not want to lie to him. I wanted only truth to exist between us. The very fact that I kept silent about my appearance, though, seemed a lie.

He groped his own face. "Am I torn?"

"Yes."

"Hideous?"

How ironic he should ask that question, above all others. "No," I said quickly. "You are merely—changed."

"My eyes—"

"The blood has clotted. Let me sponge it away, that we may find out what you can see. But, Kenzie—I am also changed. While Lady Margaret was here, she found the mirror—the one you brought me. She then knew someone else had been here and, furious, she cast a spell on me. She has altered me mightily, just as those thorns have altered you. I—I would ask you to be prepared when you look upon me."

Now he reached out and touched my face. But his fingertips, well torn, must have been inadequate for the job, because he shook his head.

"I am prepared, RapAnn."

But he could not see me. When I unwound the stiffened bandage and sponged away the dried blood, his eyelids lay shredded. And, most terrible of all, the eyes beneath had been pierced through.

****

"Lie quietly," I bade Kenzie as I bustled around the room, doing everything in my power to make him comfortable. Outside, rain continued to crash down. I'd

145

closed one shutter completely and left the other open just a crack for light. I felt sick and unsteady, full of grief yet determined not to shed any more tears.

He deserved better of me. He deserved strength and courage to match his own.

"RapAnn, come sit with me."

"You should eat. Could you manage some porridge?"

He gave a wry laugh. "I hated that stuff when I left here, and do no' doubt I will hate it still."

"We have little else." If he stayed—and I could scarcely send him away in his present condition—we would have to share what little fare Lady Margaret's magic continued to provide. Two, living as one.

"You need to regain your strength."

"Aye."

I brought the bowl and the single spoon. After several spoonsful, however, he pushed it away. "You have it."

"Not now. Kenzie, does it hurt?"

"Some—no' as bad as it did. The wounds sting. My eyes do burn."

"I think the thorns carry poison." The scratches I'd suffered while tending him yesterday felt enflamed. "Tell me what befell you after you left here. And how it is you returned to me."

"'Tis a long tale, RapAnn."

"What do we have but time?"

He began slowly, like a man describing a dream.

"I will ha' you know, I did not intend to go very far, RapAnn. I meant to linger in the forest and come right back to you as soon as that witch had left, and my presence could no longer endanger ye. But the forest, through which I ha' passed so many times while hunting, changed on me. I swear that it did. Or mayhap 'twas I who lost my sense o' direction. Do ye remember that old party game we played as wee children, wherein you are blindfolded and spun about?"

"No." I had played no such games.

"That is how it felt. The very trees seemed to shift around me. I could no' tell north fra' south, east fra' west. I could no' find the clearing. I must have searched for days."

"Magic," I breathed. "She wanted to make certain you could not find your way back to me."

"At last I emerged from the damned forest, only to find I was back in my father's lands. I went home. They were that glad to see me—"

His voice died away, a thing so unusual in him it made me stare. Kenzie, as I'd learned, was firstly a forthright man. His virtues lay in his steadiness, cheer, and honesty.

Now, I sensed the lack of all three.

"What is it, Kenzie?"

He clasped my hand in his, our fingers interlacing once more in that easy way they always had.

"My family—they expected me to resume my old life. Enough adventuring, Father said. Time to settle down."

"You wed with Anastacia," I guessed.

"No." He shook his head violently. "But our wedding is set for three weeks hence, RapAnn. I will have to leave you and once more return home."

Chapter Twenty

Can a life be lived in a day? Can it be lived, complete, in three short weeks?

I am here to tell you it can.

What followed for me—for me and Kenzie together—proved it. We had so little. But during those precious days and nights, we had everything.

Consciously, determinedly, we packed into those days the experiences we knew we should always cherish. I had all I could ask.

During the balance of that first day, we shared our stories with one another. He told me how his restlessness and longing for me would not allow him any ease, all the winter through. How he'd felt as if his heart had been left behind, here in the tower. His conviction that, whatever else happened, he must first return to me.

But the way back was as hard to find as had been the way out. And when he did at last reach the clearing—what had been the clearing—he encountered the evil vines.

"I heard ye singing," he related. "And I followed the sound. At first, when I came upon that wall of vines, I slashed at them with my sword. But whenever I hit a thorn, it dulled the blade. Next, I used my knife, but the same thing soon happened. Once that blade also became useless, the vines moved in and surrounded me.

"I could still hear your sweet voice. I followed it like a beacon and forced my way through, though it became more and more difficult the nearer to the tower I came. I could no' see. But I could hear ye. I believe I could always hear ye, RapAnn, the whole time I was awa'."

"Kenzie," I asked then, "how may you ever leave here? How force your way back through those vines?"

"I do not know. Let us no' think about it yet."

And he kissed me. That kiss contained all the warmth of old, it burned steady as a fire beside which I might sustain myself. It made nothing of the changes, or the fact that I was no longer the bonny girl with whom he'd fallen in love.

A harbinger of things to come.

For yes, our relationship thereafter changed, crossed a line over which we'd never, in the past, dared to step. Perhaps it happened because his need was so great, as was mine. Perhaps because the best comfort we could find lay in one another's arms. Whatever the reason, on the third night after his return, I gave myself to Kenzie completely, as a woman can only give herself to the man she loves. And in doing so, I found a completeness of which I'd only ever dreamed.

What is truth? It seemed I'd been searching for it all my life. But now I found it in a lie. For as he loved me, Kenzie called me beautiful, over and over again. And even though I'd told him I was changed, I fell into that lie, and did not seek further to correct him.

Can love defeat pain? Kenzie still suffered much from his wounds, so dire and numerous. But when we made love, he rose above that suffering. Can love heal the heart? I think so, for our two hearts became one and beat the more strongly for it. For the first time, I stopped worrying about the future.

Sometimes when Kenzie and I lay together on the tiny cot—woefully inadequate for the purpose—he would stroke my face. His fingertips had healed, and he ran them across my cheeks as if seeking to discover the changes of which I'd told him. How difficult I found it, keeping still while I waited for him to discover my ugliness.

But then he would murmur, "Beautiful lass," and he would kiss me.

More often still did he stroke my hair, which had not changed. He would comb it out with his fingers and murmur of his love for me.

As it always does, time passed. He healed, and as he did, so did I.

One night as we lay together on the cot with the fire burning low beside us and the shutters set ajar against the summer rain, I asked him, "What would happen if you did not go home?"

I could hear the longing in my own voice. How can I express how I wanted him to stay? With every breath, I did, and each heartbeat.

He must have heard it also, for he paused long before he replied, "It would break my father's heart. And I love him, RapAnn. He is dear to me."

"Yes, I know." I understood the width and breadth of Kenzie's heart, and how many people he loved. For me, however, there was only him.

"I love him," Kenzie reiterated, "but no' the way I love ye, RapAnn. That is different, like nothing I've ever known. 'Tis need, even more than affection, that's brought me back to you."

"Yes." I'd felt that need, every moment he'd been away. And I feared its return with his renewed absence. "But, Kenzie, I do not see how you can make your way home again, even with the highest intentions. If you are not able to see—how fight your way through the thorns?"

"I keep hoping my sight will return."

"Yes."

I bathed his eyes daily with the water from the ewer. As I'd suspected, it must have magical properties, for his wounds had healed swiftly indeed.

But so far, his sight had not returned.

"RapAnn," he told me, "I do no' intend to abandon ye. When I go, I will find a way to release you from this prison, and I will come back for you."

And if he returned to me it would be as a man married to another—his imprisonment as certain as my own. I began to say so, but stopped when he kissed me. We made love there on the tiny cot and while we did, every other consideration flew away.

One morning I awoke to discover he did not share the cot with me. A strange sound filled my ears, a long rasp that repeated over and over again.

I sat up to find morning light flooding the room. Kenzie sat near the window, even though he could not use the light, scraping the blade of his sword across the stone embrasure.

"Whatever are you doing?"

He raised his face at the sound of my voice. Most of his cuts had now healed. A few scars dotted his face and more marked his hands. His brown eyes—always so steady and sane—looked clouded, for they bore the trauma of their injuries.

"I am attempting to sharpen my sword." He spoke the obvious.

Just like that, my world cracked open. I'd done my best to live in the moment, to exist in his love for me. But, as ever, time—for good or ill—had betrayed me. It now brought grief to me once again.

"How many days left?" I asked. For nay, I'd dared not keep track.

He grimaced. "Five. Only five days. I must prepare."

"But Kenzie, you can't possibly brave that tangle below, not while you still cannot see."

He merely shook his brown head.

"I do not understand how you might suppose to make it back home."

"To be truthful, RapAnn, neither do I." Carefully, he laid aside the sword. Kenzie was always careful with objects now, placing them so he might easily find them again.

He slid across the floor to me and captured my hands.

"List to me, lass. I do no' want to leave ye. This ye must believe."

I said nothing in reply, though my fingers clenched his, hard.

"'Tis only duty takes me away."

But, my heart cried, what of me? I had never come first with anyone. My own parents had traded me away to pay a debt. Lady Margaret would have carelessly gifted me to her friend. She had abandoned me here, to live on a meager measure of magic.

I wanted to matter to someone, to matter *most*.

Yet, my heart whispered even before Kenzie spoke,

I must indeed matter to him. He'd fought his way back to me, battled across a nearly impenetrable barrier, at great cost.

What more could I ask of him?

To stay. To make his life wherever I might be, even here in this prison.

"I will fight my way out, even as I fought my way in."

"You go to wed Anastacia."

He hesitated. "I mean to speak to my father about that. You must understand, RapAnn, if I could break that betrothal, I would. But my father made the agreement with her father, and 'tis no' mine to break.

"If he will hear me, if he listens to what, to him, must sound a wild tale—just another o' my mad adventures—he may be willing to break his promise. But think on it, RapAnn. A beautiful lass in a tower, kept there by enchantment, sustained by magic. Who would believe it?"

"No one," I agreed. And the king would not be pleased his son returned to him blinded. What chance did I have? I sagged where I sat.

Kenzie jostled my hands. "I will return to you—I will return for you, RapAnn, whether he suspends the marriage obligation or no'. I will see you rescued. And I want to say—" Here he broke off, as if seeking the proper words. "'Tis you who possess my heart, you who are my true wife. D'ye understand? In my heart, 'tis so. If I am forced to wed wi' Anastacia, 'twill be a marriage in name only."

That was not fair to the girl—the thought burst across my mind—any more than me being imprisoned here. How could it be just or right for Anastacia to accept in marriage one who would never love her?

Yet such marriages of state must occur frequently.

What if, my traitorous mind whispered, he fell in love with her after the fact? What if he forgot about me?

No—no! I needed to believe in Kenzie. I must believe, even when it seemed impossible.

I wetted my lips. "And, Kenzie, what about after? What if by some miracle you do make your way through those vines and reach home, even though you cannot see…what if you wed Anastacia, and return for me? Win my way free of here, somehow—what becomes of us then?"

"Why, I will take you home, of course. See you settled somewhere safe, comfortable, and out of Lady Margaret's reach. We shall still be able to see one another, even if I am wed."

That made me shudder. "Others will see me," I whispered. "They will tell you how—how much I am changed from the girl you first beheld."

"RapAnn!" He shook my hands slightly. "You are the girl I first beheld. You were beautiful before I went blind, and you will be when we grow old together. D'ye suppose I care for aught anyone might say?"

I cared. And at that moment, the possibility of us growing old together seemed ten worlds away.

Chapter Twenty-One

Those final five days passed far too swiftly. Kenzie sharpened his sword and his knife and continued to bathe his eyes in the water from the ewer.

His sight did not return.

Me, I marshaled my arguments, convinced that when it came down to it, I could persuade him not to leave. It seemed such madness, a blind man attempting to negotiate the perils that lay below and trying to make his way home. Breaking my heart in the process.

I lined up the words to say, in my mind. And when the last morning came, a clear, warm, and beautiful morning filled with birdsong, I went and knelt beside him where he sat.

Immediately, he stopped what he was doing, placed his knife in its sheath, and laid his warm hand against my cheek.

It felt like a blessing, that touch, one without which I could no longer live.

"What is it, RapAnn?"

He could not see me. He did not have to. I gazed into his beloved face, and all my carefully garnered words threatened to desert me.

I captured his hand between both of mine. "Please, Kenzie, do not go."

"RapAnn, I—"

"I love you." Though I certainly owned that

emotion, at least toward him, I'd never yet spoken those words, not to anyone. Nay, not even to him when we lay together, so exquisitely joined, and our hearts beat as one. I'd had no one to love, ever, but him. And the thought of losing him terrified me.

His expression warmed and light came into his empty eyes. "And I love ye, bonnie lass. 'Tis why I go fra' ye now."

"It cannot be. If you loved me, you would stay with me. You go for the sake of duty, to please your father—and to wed Anastacia."

"For those reasons, aye, but even more to win a future for you. There is none for ye here, my love. There is only continual imprisonment."

"Enlightened by your presence."

"'Tis imprisonment, all the same."

"Kenzie—all I need is you. Nothing, nothing more."

"My dearest lass, ye ha' lived on so very little, for so long. Let me offer ye more. Allow me to battle my way out with that cause as my shield. I will no' leave ye trapped here for the rest o' your days."

He did not understand—or he did not believe—I needed only him to survive. Claiming the very best intentions, he would take that one thing from me. Better, quicker, and easier to drive the newly sharpened dagger into my heart.

"You have tried before to find a way to free me. You consulted with your friend, who understands magic. There is no way."

"I will yet find one, even if I need to come back here with a troop o' men and take down this tower, stone from stone."

If he came back at all.

"But, RapAnn, I canna' do it alone. You must help me by keeping faith. Believe in me, and wait for me."

My whole life had consisted of waiting, so it seemed. Now he asked me to do it again when I could not even imagine the outcome, or the life that would follow should his wild endeavor succeed. Would he install me in his father's kingdom in some capacity, even while wed to another? Could such an existence possibly hold any room for happiness?

"Here, lass, do no' take on so." He leaned in and kissed me. A kiss of promise, he no doubt intended it to be, but he must have tasted my despair.

"RapAnn," he asked, "can ye no' ha' faith I will return to ye?"

I wept. "I do not see how."

"Love brought me hence once and let me battle my way through to you. Love will bring me again. Trust me, RapAnn. Trust in our love. 'Tis the strongest magic there is."

What could I say to that? I did not want to toss such a declaration back in his face. But I will admit: on that bright, sweet morning, I could not do as he asked and believe.

Yet I helped him prepare. I wrapped a thick fold of fabric from my sacrificed dress around his eyes for protection, and more strips about his hands like gauntlets.

At the last, he kissed me again and asked, "RapAnn, will ye let down your hair for me?"

I did so, weeping.

"And will ye sing for me?"

"Sing?"

"So I may strike a path away. And in the days to come, keep singing. Your voice is what will lead me back again."

Sing, with a broken heart? I did not think it possible, no more than the birds sang in winter.

But that, and only that, could bring him back to me. "I will."

He kissed me one last time. Then I wound my hair around the iron hook and let it over the sill. He climbed down and disappeared from view.

But I heard him still—I heard him as he hacked his way steadily through the bitter-smelling vines. And I sang to guide him on his path, the path away from me.

****

I will admit, I descended into darkness after Kenzie left, even deeper than that which beset me the first time I lost his company. For days I did not rise from my cot. I took neither food nor drink, and the water in the ewer brimmed right to the top, though Lady Margaret's magic kept it from spilling over.

I did not weep, for I had spent all my tears. I thought much, however, on my life, traced the path of it—every step as thorny as what Kenzie negotiated—much as I have related it here.

Kenzie was right about one thing. I had lived very long on very little. My world, so it seemed, had grown ever narrower. It had narrowed, also, the scope of my imagination.

I could not conceive of anything beyond the stone room, the cot, and the pitcher.

Kenzie assured me there was a world outside this place, and I knew there had been a world—if limited— on Lady Margaret's estate. But neither seemed real.

Reality had become the touch of Kenzie's hand. The beat of his heart beneath my cheek in the night. The steady warmth of his presence.

Gone, all gone.

I needed to believe he would keep the promise made in love and return to me. Easier to believe Lady Margaret would come instead, intent upon inflicting some new cruelty.

Neither occurred. Days dragged by in the way they always do, and I failed to sing. Neither did I comb out my hair, which grew tangled. I did sit beside the window sometimes, listening, but heard only the wind in the trees and vines. The leaves began to turn color, and the birds flew south.

I dreamed I could fly also. I stood on the windowsill and spread my arms like wings, and launched myself from my toes. I let the air currents carry me up and out over the sea of green vines.

I awoke to find I did, indeed, stand on the edge of the stone casement, teetering on the verge of a plummet. For an instant I considered letting go, giving in to the despair.

Then Kenzie's face swam before my mind's eye. What if I dashed myself down, to be torn among the vines below? Or I might fall onto the place he'd hacked open when last he descended. For the vines had not yet had time to fill that in. It snaked away around the bottom of the tower and took a path my eyes could not pursue.

If he did return, I did not want him to find me lying broken and bloodied.

My traitorous heart insisted he would not return.

Yes, but if he did?

My love for him, and nothing more, made me back down from the embrasure and move away to safety.

Chapter Twenty-Two

That autumn, I made a curious discovery. Not only was I imprisoned in the stone tower, I was imprisoned also in my own head. Perhaps I always had been.

When you think about it, so it is for each of us. We come into the world, born into myriad situations. I, traded away. Kenzie, born to privilege. Others seemingly destined to lives lived as peasants, merchants, craftsmen, or thieves.

But it is not so. It only *seems*. For if the trials of my life had taught me one thing, it is that none of us ever leaves the tiny room we inhabit—that of our mind, our own perspective.

Lady Margaret may have limited me, yes. At her manor, she had taken from me all she could, each item she supposed I needed to survive.

Yet I'd survived. I'd been strong enough for that.

After she brought me here, life had continued the process she'd begun. I lost all. Yet did I remain.

Over those terrible weeks the autumn after Kenzie left me a second time, I pondered that fact. The strength of it may well have saved me. On the other hand, I may have merely slid over the precipice into madness—I could no longer tell.

I spoke to myself on a regular basis, spoke as I once had to Kenzie, or to some other not seen. I spoke to the RapAnn within, she who had always been my companion and could not abandon me. She always listened. She did not care that my slippers had worn through, my face had been ruined, and my hair hung in dreadful tangles. She fed me songs to sing. She murmured to me in the dark of night, when despair grew so thick I could not see. Like me, she had lost all hope. But I knew she would remain with me throughout eternity.

Did I live for her? I cannot say, but by mid-autumn I knew I had another reason to live. For I felt new life stir, inside.

I might have been an innocent when first shut away from the world, but I knew how babies were conceived and came into the world. Indeed, I had suspected the occurrence, since the habits of my body had changed. But the fluttering in my belly gave proof of it.

I wonder, can you imagine how I felt? I was to bear a child, the child of the man I loved and believed gone from me forever.

Here, alone.

But a piece of him—a precious likeness, perhaps—would give me something to hold.

How could I raise a child here in this barren place? How feed and clothe it? The doubts and questions were manifold.

Yet…yet I had not lost *all*.

That thought made me weep. I may well have lost Kenzie. Fate had given me someone to take his place in my heart.

Thereafter, contrasting thoughts haunted me. Would the enchanted provisions prove enough for two, as the child grew? What if Lady Margaret returned, condemned me as a harlot, and took the child from me, even as she'd taken me from my parents?

That I could not endure.

What if Kenzie returned and took me from this place, to his father's kingdom? How might the king welcome me when I came bearing his son's illegitimate child?

I discussed it with she who dwelt inside my head, for she sometimes saw things much more clearly than I.

Wait, she bade me.

The eternal stricture. I had no choice but to wait, yet each passing day brought the child closer to being born. I loved it already, with fierce fervor.

Mine. This one thing, I would let no one take from me, however I had to fight.

Winter came, first with soft snowflakes that dusted the vines below, falling on their stems, which stayed eternally green, though the blood-red roses had long since gone. Then came the winds and storms that turned the stones of the tower to ice. The fire seemed to burn very low, yet I felt warmed from within.

I began singing to my child. Nay, let me correct that—I sang to Kenzie's child, as once I had to him. I rested beside the meager fire and combed out my hair, which now spread all around my feet, and I thought about the child being born.

Boy or girl? It did not matter. A wee lad like his father would be a comfort, but so would a lass who looked the way Kenzie remembered me. Or the babe might take a bit from each of us, a reminder that we had loved.

Did I truly go mad that winter? I suppose, being alone so much over the years of my life, I'd long flirted with that condition. Or perhaps I saw things clearly for the very first time.

****

How quiet the forest on a winter's morning. Indeed, the way I calculated it, we were not far off from spring, the worst of the harsh weather passed.

On this particular morning I sat with the shutters ajar, singing softly to my child, who stirred, very lively within me. And I paused when my ear caught a sound.

You must understand, sound carries far on such a cold, clear morning. And, with the birds flown, and the trees standing still, nothing moved at that time.

I cocked my head—very like one of those birds—and rose slowly. I went to the window and swung the shutters wide.

Of course I could see nothing. Just acres of treetops, skeletal branches reaching for the sky, with the vines lurking below.

A hunting party, I decided, though my heart lurched painfully. Defiant of the cold, I leaned out and listened.

The sounds did, indeed, travel far in the still air, and were nothing I recognized. Not the clatter of horses' hooves but a strange, rhythmic thumping. And voices.

Were those voices?

What if Lady Margaret came? What if she'd conceived of some new cruelty for me? What if, finding me swollen with child, she flew into a cold fury and dashed me from the window?

Hush, said the RapAnn within. *Hush and sing. Sing.*

I sang. I sat there in the cold air from the window and sang every song I knew, while the sun climbed into the sky overhead and the odd sounds grew ever nearer.

By noon, I could tell that, indeed, there were voices. Men, calling to one another. A great hacking, as of axes being wielded. And then, and then—

I saw the vines below me, at the very edge of the forest, shiver. I was on my feet by then, once more leaning out perilously far.

Kenzie? I longed to call to him, but dared not. What if these were the voices of Lady Margaret's guards?

A path appeared across what used to be the clearing. The vines at the foot of the tower crashed and fell. They went down in great swathes. As they did, the enchantment seemed to fall away with them. I looked down and saw a crew of men, all dressed alike in dark green tunics and leather leggings. They wielded bright-bladed axes as they came, hacking at the vines. I went hot and cold by turns. Rescue? Or another catastrophe?

Then I caught the sound of a single voice among the many. "Can ye see the tower?"

I am not ashamed to admit my knees failed me. I sank down with my fingers still clutching the casement and rested my forehead against the cold stone.

Oh, I wanted—needed—to see him. Somehow, I found the strength to stand and look out again.

"We see the tower, Prince Kenzie." A husky voice, that one, from a member of the stout crew.

"Is she there? Can ye see her, perhaps in the window?"

Not awaiting an answer, a figure pushed forward, straining his face upward though, to be sure, he could see nothing.

"RapAnn? RapAnn, are ye there?"

"Kenzie."

The word came soft from my lips, even as my fingers curled against the stone. For there he stood with his scarred, earnest face and his brown hair shining in the sun.

"Kenzie!"

He started forward, joy suffusing his features. But the men caught him back again.

"Prince Kenzie, wait."

We both waited while the men hauled away the last of the vines. Mere moments it must have been, though they seemed to take an age. At last the men stood aside, and Kenzie rushed forward.

"RapAnn, let down your hair!"

I did so, with clumsily eager hands. And he climbed up to me, my one love, restoring the light to my world.

Chapter Twenty-Three

In most tellings of my tale, that is where the story ends. Some fool says something like, "So the handsome prince rescued RapAnn, and they all lived happily ever after."

But how could it be so? I ask you, how could the tale end when it had barely begun?

Kenzie did climb up the rope of my hair while his men waited below. Instantly, we reached for one another. I wanted to prove to myself he was real, and he of course, could not see me save by touch.

He drew me fast into his arms, enfolded me, and held me tight.

For those first moments, nothing else mattered. Once, I had lost all. But in that instant, all was restored to me.

Breathless, smelling of the cold outdoors and of his own dear scent, he kissed me. Tears stood in his poor, blinded eyes when at last he drew away.

"RapAnn, my love, I am that sorry it took so long to return to you. Are ye well?"

Was I? Half mad, abandoned so long with only the part of me, inside, that represented my remaining strength, I scarcely knew. But I said, "It doesn't matter, Kenzie, not now."

Well, one thing did matter. By touch, he located the swell of his child, caught between us. His eyes filled first with wonder, and next with joy.

"RapAnn—"

"As you can feel, I have not been quite alone."

"Och, my bonny girl, my amazing lass! I did no' dream—"

I reached up and trapped his face between my palms. My heart thudded within me. "Are you glad?"

"Glad! That does not express it."

"But—but Anastacia…you must be wed to her by now." I tried to imagine it, a state wedding when he'd returned home. Had he spent the long winter in his new wife's bed? Might she too carry his child? A legitimate child, unlike mine. Oh, how could I face it?

His expression sobered. "Of that, lass, we must speak. First, I mean to get you out of this prison, once and for all."

Out. Can I begin to explain how the prospect frightened me? The tower had long been my prison, yes. And it had kept me safe from a world I might be ill equipped to face.

Kenzie assured me, "I ha' come well prepared. There are blankets, food, and even medicine below. My men stand ready to assist us. We did ha' to hack our way in, and no easy task it was."

"I heard, I heard."

"The vines ha' grown right into the forest, a proper tangle. But at this time o' the year, as we discovered, they become brittle and fall awa wi' a mere kiss of the axe. My men ha' made a braw trail, and we can follow it awa' from this place."

"But—but," I objected, let it be admitted with an edge of despair, "I cannot get down. And you cannot toss me down," if that he did envision, "for fear of harm to the babe."

He caressed the swell of my belly reverently. "That we will no' do." A sudden smile transfigured his face. "There is another way."

Why could he not just stay here with me, safe and warm as we had been? Must he take me out into the terrifying world? I suppose so, for his men waited below, and his life waited—all those he loved, like his brothers and sisters, his father, and Anastacia who, like me, no doubt loved him.

If I did, indeed, love him, I could not keep him here. But oh, after so much time, had I the courage to face a life beyond?

I drew a shaky breath. "How, Kenzie? You get up and down by climbing my hair. The hook rejects all else. And I cannot climb my own hair, can I?"

His smile broadened. "Och but, my love, aye—you can."

****

"Do ye recall the fellow of whom I told ye before—Master Justin?" Kenzie asked as he used a rope he'd brought to haul up a number of items from below. Warm clothing, and food, and several closed packs. I noticed he moved with much more assurance than when he'd left. He must have grown accustomed to his blindness.

"Yes," I replied. "I remember. You said he was familiar with Lady Margaret's reputation and knew much of magic."

"Aye. He has become my fast friend, as well as my advisor. We pondered long and hard these many months past for a solution to your dilemma."

Kenzie turned to me. "But first, I need to explain to

ye why it took me so long to return. Here," he unfurled a warm cloak from a bundle. "Put this on and tak' something to eat, while I tell the tale."

I didn't think I could eat. My stomach fluttered near as wildly as his child, beneath my heart, but I sat obediently with an oatcake in my hand.

He paced in front of me as he spoke.

"The journey home was hard. You canna' know, RapAnn, what it took for me to leave ye, to aim my steps away while your songs died awa' behind. Those accursed vines, which I could no' see, tore at me and snagged my clothing over and over again. The fabric o' your gown, though, which ye tied over my eyes and my hands, must ha' carried some enchantment, for the thorns never penetrated my face or hands.

"A hundred times I despaired, thinking I would no' make it through. I very nearly turned back to you. But I knew if I did, we would both be trapped here, mayhap forever."

I might favor being trapped, especially with him, but did not say so.

"Once I reached the forest, it went better, though still not easily. I lost much time traveling in circles, for I could hear your voice no more, and so could not get a clear direction. At length I stumbled out onto a road and met wi' a carter. He carried me into the kingdom, and home."

"Your father must have been overjoyed to see you. And—and Anastacia."

"I missed the wedding day. And I was very ill when I got home, out of my head with fever. The castle physicians later said poison from the thorns must have worked its way into my blood."

"Oh, my poor love."

"I lay senseless for some time. When I could, I told my family about you. My parents, as may well be imagined, were sore distressed by my blindness. Och, how my mother wept!"

"And—and Anastacia?" I imagined her tending him, fussing over him even as I would have done.

Kenzie's expression turned bleak. "I will speak of that anon."

He did not want to break it to me, I thought—that the wedding had taken place after he recovered, that perhaps he had another child on the way.

That, if I journeyed to his father's kingdom with him, I would be shuffled out of sight, perhaps even shut away as I had been at the manor, a mere afterthought.

He smiled sadly. "It took me much longer than it should to regain my strength. 'Tis the first time I've been so happy to ha' so many sisters. They were gey kind to me."

"I am glad." And I was, for I loved him.

"As soon as I could get out of bed, I consulted with Justin. He studied every spell book he had and entertained no end of wild ideas." Kenzie's eyes gleamed. "Then he happened upon the answer. And och, what a simple answer it is!"

"Tell me," I begged with equal parts eagerness and apprehension.

He stopped pacing and reached for my hands. "The only way in or, indeed, out o' here, barring Lady Margaret using her magic, is the act of climbing your hair, aye?"

"And thus, I cannot climb down."

"That, RapAnn, is only true if the rope of hair

remains attached to your bonny head." He furnished the statement triumphantly, and could not see me stare at him in dawning horror.

"You do not mean—"

"We maun cut it off." Letting go of my hands, he fumbled in a nearby pack and withdrew a pair of golden shears. "See here. These did Justin have made, and prepared for the exact task. They bear a spell against enchantment, just in case Lady Margaret left a spell on your hair, also."

He fell to his knees at my feet.

"RapAnn, RapAnn, ye maun cut off your hair."

Chapter Twenty-Four

Cut off my hair. It might seem a simple—yes, even a brilliant—solution. Braid the stuff tight, make a golden rope out of it, and chop it off. Affix it to the iron hook—for only my hair would attach there—and pray it would hold long enough for us to descend.

Cut off my hair.

But Kenzie loved my hair. He had reveled in the length of it when we lay together, and combed it with adoring fingers. He'd buried his face in it. It was my one remaining claim to beauty.

My face, ruined. My body no longer lithe but swelled and ripe.

Did he expect me to sacrifice my hair also, on the chance it would allow us a way down?

I stood there, suffused by distress and knowing I could not speak any objection to him. He'd come through so much to make his way back to me. He came with such gladness at having brought a solution.

Could I bleat out a protest that smacked of sheer vanity?

He covered my silence with excited explanations. "I can scarce believe, RapAnn, neither you nor I thought of it sooner. If only we had, it would have saved so much—all these months you've spent here alone, imprisoned. We might have left together before ever Lady Margaret rooted those vines."

Which would have prevented his blindness. And had I left with him the first time he went, Lady Margaret would never have been able to charge me with his presence and alter my appearance so dreadfully.

I owed him this. I should chop off the length of my hair without a murmur, and be joyful in it.

Yet—yet!

What would his people, some of whom waited even now down below, think when they saw me? Shorn, great with child, and bearing the face I'd glimpsed in the glass.

Would his people laugh and scoff at him? Would his family secretly—or not so secretly—jeer at me?

I stepped to the window and looked out. Kenzie's men took a well-deserved rest from their labors, sitting in the area they'd worked to clear of vines, and sharing refreshments from their packs. None of them so much as glanced up at me. I did not want them to—I couldn't bear to see the expression that would come to their eyes.

Maybe I should stay here, in the tower.

That thought terrified me, because it felt so powerful. I'd spent most my life longing for freedom. Now, for the first time, it came on offer, but it also came with a condition I could not bear to face.

"What is it, RapAnn? Ye do no' seem as happy as I expected."

Yes, he knew me—the very warp and weft of me, even as I knew him.

Swiftly, I turned to him. "I am glad to see you, Kenzie, so glad. Never doubt it."

I stepped into his arms once more, and we kissed.

Almost did that persuade me. Nearly did that make everything else go away.

He brushed my cheek with gentle fingers. "Tell me, my love."

I whispered, "I am frightened. What will happen to me out in the world? What will happen to us?"

Comprehension flooded his sightless eyes. "Aye, I should ha' thought, and told ye at once. I ha' it all set for ye, RapAnn—a quiet cottage for the time being, with a kindhearted young maid to look after ye. Ye need, at first, see only me, if that will make ye comfortable."

A kept woman—a hideous one.

"And what will your wife say to that?"

"My wife?"

"Anastacia."

He began to laugh—not with mirth so much as sadness. "Sit, love. Let me explain." He once more took both my hands in his. "When I fought my way back out o' here last autumn, I left my heart behind. Ye maun understand that."

Tears started to my eyes. "Yes."

"The whole way back, I wondered what I should do about that marriage. My father is king and had made a solemn agreement on my behalf. He has been very good to me, and I love him. Duty lay strongly upon me. But—there are times the heart speaks loudly indeed.

"All the while I journeyed home, I heard your voice inside my head. I will tell you fairly, for I will never lie to you, even when I reached home I had no' made up my mind what to do about it. Then I fell so ill. The wedding was postponed. I could no' speak o' it with my father, nor did I see Anastacia for weeks."

"Oh."

He shook his head slightly. "I should ha' had more faith in what my heart already knew. You and I are meant to be together, so I do swear. Halves o' the same coin. I feel complete only when I am wi' ye."

"And I, with you," I admitted. "But Anastacia—"

"At the beginning of winter, my father began to speak of rescheduling the wedding, for the winter solstice possibly. That is when Anastacia's father sent word." He squeezed my hands hard. "Anastacia decided she could not countenance tying herself for life to a blind man. There will be no wedding, at least no' between Anastacia and me."

****

There are moments in life when everything pauses and, like a river in flood, takes off in a different direction. The first time I refused Jeremiah Cole had been one such, and so had the day Lady Margaret brought me to the tower.

Such moments, when they arrived, called up all the strength within me, and required endurance I didn't know I possessed. It might be fair to say they had made me the woman I now was.

As had my love for this man who clutched my hands so tightly, and gazed at me with hope in his blind eyes.

Could I do this thing—for him? Could I face the stares, the exposure and condemnation?

All my life I'd been searching for the truth, combing through the layers of illusion that surrounded me, just as I combed through the tangles in my hair. Now it all rested on one question.

Did I love Kenzie more than I feared exposing

myself to others and their censure?

I whispered, "You want to marry me?"

"Aye, RapAnn. 'Tis all I ha' wanted since I met you. And I long for it doubly now that you carry my child. Say yes, RapAnn, please."

I drew my hands from his and pressed them to my face. "What will people say? You bringing back a woman from nowhere, a woman already great with your child."

"I do no' care what people say."

"And one—one who looks as I do."

"RapAnn, you are beautiful."

"You say that only because you cannot see me."

"I see you constantly, in my mind. I see ye wi' my heart. My family and the people of our kingdom will accept you, for the love of me or—more rightly—for your own bonnie self."

I tried to imagine it, a state wedding with hundreds of people looking on. The sneers and stares of condemnation that Kenzie could not see. Nowhere, nowhere to hide.

Yet he offered me his heart, whole. I could certainly ask no more.

"RapAnn," he urged, "let down your hair for me one last time, and come awa' wi' me into a new life."

Chapter Twenty-Five

I took the golden shears into my own hands and examined them. Enchanted, Kenzie said they were. They looked wickedly sharp, and their blades winked in the light coming through the window.

I had already combed out my hair and braided it tightly, which took some time. The men down below had finished their repast, and now moved about. Kenzie also grew restless. He wanted to be away by nightfall. I could not say I blamed him.

Yet as I stood regarding the golden shears a thought blazed through my mind. I had already lost so much. Must my fate command even this?

"RapAnn," Kenzie said.

"Yes. I will do it."

I opened the shears and positioned them beside my ear, just above the place where the plait began.

I cut.

The hair screamed.

It terrified me so I dropped the shears. Kenzie, who could see nothing—poor man—started and swore. I heard the men down below exclaim.

"What was that?"

"Prince Kenzie, are ye well?"

Both of us ignored them.

The strands of hair I'd cut cried out as I severed them. In pain? Hard to tell. But the hair had my voice—

the one I raised when I sang.

By cutting my hair, I severed a very part of me, past from future.

But did I want to hang onto the past?

The question had me snatching up the shears again.

"All right, it's all right," I told Kenzie, and all at once it was.

I cut and hacked that braid from my head. Brutal I was with it, and the hair screamed, wailed, and moaned.

I heeded it no longer.

The last shrieks died away as the plait hit the floor. I stood with the golden shears in my hands and stared at the plait. Separate from me, for the first time ever.

To Kenzie I said, "It is done."

"Ah, RapAnn—I did no' expect—"

"Never mind." He had sacrificed his sight for me. I could shed this.

He groped his way to the window and reassured his men before turning once more to me.

"The moment of truth, my love. Will it affix to the hook?"

I laid the shears aside, gathered up my hair, and carried it to the window. The hook had been there so long, in all weathers, that it had rusted, and now appeared scabby and pock-marked. But it had served to pull Kenzie up. I had to believe it would serve us one last time.

Lifting my hair—no mean feat now that it lay free—I looped it around the hook and tied it tight. The individual strands curled around the metal as if they were alive, and gripped tenaciously.

I told Kenzie, "It will hold."

"Thank God, RapAnn. Thank God!"

By touch, he gathered up the things he'd brought and dropped them down to the men below before turning to me.

"Are ye ready, lass?"

Was I?

"You go first," I told him.

"Nay. We go together or no' at all. I will carry ye."

"How?"

"If ye think I will risk letting you dash yoursel' and our bairn against those stones, ye are much mistaken. I will carry ye," he repeated it like a vow.

He insisted I loop my arms about his neck and hold on securely. He wrapped one arm around me and twisted the other hand in my hair. Backing over the sill, he used his feet against the stones and we went down.

Together.

Willing hands received us and glad exclamations abounded. I trembled so badly I could barely stand, when my feet met the ground, and I did not want to look into the faces of Kenzie's men for fear of beholding their reactions to my appearance.

I kept my eyes cast down. But as they loaded their packs, I did glance back up at the tower, searching.

The window stood open and the interior looked very dark. My hair still snaked down in a trail of bright gold, and for an instant I felt the wrench of terrible loss.

Then Kenzie took me by the hand. "Come, lass. Awa' from this dreadful place."

Kenzie's men proved very kind to me during that difficult journey. Young fellows all, and Kenzie's contemporaries, they behaved like friends as much as like his father's guards.

One, named Daniel, had a grave, stoic nature and

treated me most politely. The other two—Anders and Bertram—were brothers and, had they not been quite so concerned with our situation, might have been the sort to tease and make jokes.

But they were concerned. It could not have been easy guiding Kenzie on what they no doubt considered a mad chase. And they had not expected to find me with child. Like young men everywhere, they treated me as if they expected I might go into labor at any moment.

Never, by any word or look, did they reveal how appalled they must be by my appearance. Courteous and respectful, they barely raised their eyes to my face.

We traveled slowly, hampered both by Kenzie's blindness and my condition. The men had cut a stout trail through the vines on their way in, yet I was astonished to see how far the tangled greenery extended into the forest.

I knew, then, Lady Margaret never entertained any notion of returning. She had abandoned me to the isolation of the tower and a long, lonely demise.

I would have lived my life and died there, save for Kenzie.

That thought brought gratitude up strong in my heart. I resolved I could face anything, however painful, for his sake.

At last we emerged from the vines, and the forest. The light had already begun to fail. Still, it felt so strange having clear vistas around me on every side. I could see the hills stretching away like sleeping beasts, and the broad valley of the border. The party had left their horses here, and the beasts waited patiently, chomping the turf.

"We ride from here," Kenzie told me. "All the way

home."

Home. The prospect terrified me. Nervously, I ran my fingers through my cropped hair and sought to pull it forward enough to cover my face. I had cut it too short. I, who once had the longest hair of all, now stood woefully shorn.

I wanted to weep but would not shame Kenzie so before his men.

"I will tak' ye up on my saddle with me," Kenzie said. "My mount is used to following the others."

"How long will the journey take?"

"We will be home by morning."

****

Oh, that journey! A thousand conflicting emotions beset me on the way. My fears ran rampant, countered by the sheer pleasure of being in Kenzie's arms. He made me feel safe and sheltered, and as I told myself over and over again, that alone mattered.

We may tell ourselves any number of things in an effort to believe them. I had so little knowledge of what might occur when we reached the kingdom and sufficient imagination to provide daunting possibilities.

During our hours together in the tower, Kenzie had spoken much and fondly of his father. For the most part, King Maximillian sounded a kind man. But try as I might, I could scarce imagine him welcoming me, homeless, nameless, and certainly no beauty, in place of she whom he'd chosen as wife for his son.

The glories of the countryside, in part, distracted me. I had never ridden so far in the open, on horseback, nor had leave to watch the stars move overhead, or see the dawn come toward me as we rode eastward.

Golden, the light was. It flowed like honey across

the hills and over the land.

"Try to sleep," Kenzie murmured to me several times. "I will no' let ye fall."

I could not sleep for the dread churning inside.

At last I asked, "Are we nearly there?"

"Aye. Daniel," Kenzie called, "nearly home?"

"Indeed, Prince Kenzie," the man answered. "I see Ben Laurel just ahead."

I looked, and my eyes widened.

A stout road ran ahead of us, beside a burn which had come down from the mountain Daniel called Ben Laurel. It led to a line of tiny cottages, all well kept, and other buildings. Bathed by the soft, golden light I marked a smithy, a potter's, and a market, now quiet.

The castle, though, demanded my attention. Built of gray stone, not unlike the tower, it sat on a gentle rise and dwarfed Lady Margaret's manor the way a lofty pine might overshadow a sapling.

Sheer dismay struck me silent, yet the party, relentless, rode on.

The broad castle gates stood open, though guarded. The guardsmen saluted our party and stared curiously at me. I wanted to hide my face against Kenzie's shoulder then, for fear of shaming him.

We rode on into a wide forecourt which, even at this early hour, teemed with people. Men clad like those in our company hurried about, and women carried baskets and bundles across the way. Hounds and even a few children dashed about.

Everyone stopped to stare at us. I told myself they might show like interest for any party arriving at such an hour, yet all I saw were faces turning to me, eyes staring and lips parting as they gaped.

At my sorry appearance?

I reminded myself Kenzie could not see those glances. But he must have felt the tension grip me, for his arms tightened and he whispered, "Whisht!"

"Kenzie, I—"

"I know how strange all this must be for ye, my love. Can ye but be brave for me?"

I could. I must.

Chapter Twenty-Six

Despite the amount of time I'd spent alone during my life, I'd never considered myself a recluse. My solitude had been forced upon me, including those months in my room at Lady Margaret's manor and my years in the tower.

Now the world—Kenzie's world—came rushing upon me. Unlike the gentle beauties of the natural world I'd glimpsed while traveling, this seemed all too intense and overwhelming.

Kenzie did his best to insulate me from all of it. From the very first, when we dismounted in the forecourt and eager hands reached to lead the weary horses away, he sought to shield me. Yet everywhere I looked, I saw people staring.

How I longed for my shorn hair then, that I might hide my altered face in it. As it was, I kept my gaze lowered, so I need not read the thoughts of those I encountered. But you may be certain I felt the weight of all those stares.

"Come," Kenzie said in my ear. But before he could lead me off, a merry band suddenly poured through the main doors of the castle, much the way the burn had gushed down the side of the brae.

It took me only one or two glances to determine these must be members of Kenzie's family. For they had the look of him—stout and hearty—fairly sparkling with life, as he had been when first I met him. They possessed the same glossy brown hair and bright eyes, set wide beneath level brows.

He'd told me all their names and described their personalities also, during our long days alone together. No doubt, given a moment to catch my breath, I could have identified them. I had no such opportunity, for they fell upon us, chattering like my birds had in the spring, back at the tower.

With them came another man, tall and spare, wearing on his black hair a blue-striped bonnet that matched his vivid blue eyes.

He clapped Kenzie on the back and exclaimed, "My prince! I am that happy to see ye returned. So you ha' your prize."

A prize, me? No, he could not mean so.

Kenzie turned to him with a wide smile, and drew me close against his side. "Two prizes, Justin, as ye may well see."

Justin? This man it was who had worked tirelessly to free me, so Kenzie had said. At that realization, I took a shy glance into his face and extended my hand. "Master Justin, I am most grateful for all your efforts on my behalf."

His blue gaze inspected me swiftly—my swollen belly, my shorn hair, and lastly, my face. In the merciless, bright light of the courtyard, I stood pitilessly revealed. He must be able to see precisely what Lady Margaret's spell had done to me.

Yet his expression registered no disgust. Instead it turned warm with kindness and, perhaps, pity.

He sketched a bow. "My lady, you are welcome. I am most happy and relieved that our scheme to free you succeeded. The tresses held to the hook?"

"As you can see." Kenzie beamed.

"It is well, and I wish you every blessing."

Similar greetings and introductions continued for some time, inescapable. Face after face swam into view before my dazed eyes. Kenzie's brothers and sisters swarmed him and embraced him in turn. I saw nothing but curiosity in their eyes and, again, what I took for pity.

I swayed on my feet before Kenzie's parents appeared. They came together, and a majestic couple they did make.

King Maximillian wore a fine, fur-trimmed cape over clothing similar to Kenzie's, and had a simple golden crown on his dark head. He had the look of Kenzie about the eyes, but he guarded his expression so well, when he saw me, I could only guess at the dismay he must feel.

Kenzie's mother, the queen, proved sweet-faced and plump as a partridge, clad in a gown of gorgeous rose pink with a veil covering her brown hair. I could not miss the kindness in her eyes.

"Och, poor child," she murmured, and reached for my hands. "Kenzie, let me tak' her awa' inside, out o' all this."

Her husband gave her a bemused, and slightly reproving, glance at this. He'd already swept my belly with an all-encompassing stare, and I fancied his lips tightened.

"Son," he said to Kenzie, "we maun speak o' this."

"Aye, Father." Kenzie turned to me. "Will ye go with my mother, love? I will be wi' ye as soon as ever I can."

My heart plummeted, but I would not mark my arrival with bitter protests, especially before so many.

I accompanied the queen from the courtyard, and most of Kenzie's sisters fell in behind us.

****

The interior of the castle, like the forecourt, bustled with activity. We swept down stone corridors, and I did my best to keep my face turned away from those whom we encountered. I could hear Kenzie's sisters murmuring behind us, and after a swift look at me, Queen Rowena—for such was her name—ushered me into a chamber at the top of the stairs before turning at bay.

"Whisht, now," she told her daughters, sounding very much like Kenzie. "Allow the lass some time to collect hersel'."

They grumbled as the door shut in their faces, though I could not hide the extent of my relief when Queen Rowena turned to me.

The chamber—a lovely solar—offered every comfort, including a padded bench set before a cheerful fire. Queen Rowena led me there and urged me to sit before bringing me a chalice with her own hands.

"Here, drink."

Noting my startled glance into the cup, she smiled. "'Tis naught that can harm you—just water flavored with sloe."

I accepted the cup, and she sat down beside me. Her eyes, hazel-green and very kind, inspected me for a long moment.

"Well, Kenzie has certainly set a cat among the pigeons this time. Since he was very small, so I do assure you, he has had a tendency to do so. All my sons, aye, are dauntless and strong. Kenzie, however, usually has some reckless scheme in his head."

I could only agree it had been reckless for Kenzie to bring me here this way. I wondered if this kind woman, so obviously fond of him, knew I was to blame for his blindness. Dared I confide in her?

"Lass, what is your name?"

"RapAnn, your highness."

"And," she hesitated but an instant, "when will your babe be born?"

"I am not quite certain. I have never…never—"

"Ah. Well, as one with a great deal of experience, I should say you ha' a month or so to go. And," she asked with curiosity rather than suspicion, "you claim this to be my son's child?"

"Oh, yes, your highness."

Her lips tightened, and she studied me anew. "Such a thing is very easy to say and rather harder to prove."

"I understand how unlikely it must seem, especially…well, especially given the look of me. But this child cannot possibly belong to anyone else. You see, I was locked away in a tower, by a powerful witch." Setting the goblet aside, I pressed both hands to my face. "She did this to me."

All at once, I began to weep. The tears came thick and fast, and I could not halt them.

"There, now," Queen Rowena said meaninglessly. "That is weariness fr' the journey, no doubt, and reaction to being hauled into the courtyard before so many. Plus, a woman tends to grow emotional, so close to her time. Sit quietly a moment. I will ha' a room prepared for ye, awa' fra' all this."

She went out softly, and I drew a shaky breath.

Alone with my thoughts at last—my natural state, so it seemed. Seeking composure, I spoke silently to the RapAnn within. "She does not believe me. Why should she? She supposes me some chit appeared from nowhere, with designs on her beloved son."

I rose and went to the window of the chamber. It must face away from the busy courtyard, for I saw only a broad vista of hills and what looked like a garden below.

Another window. Another garden. Had I but exchanged my prison for a new one? It seemed I'd come full circle, and little changed.

Then Kenzie's child kicked hard inside, and I knew that this time, however it might seem, everything had changed.

Chapter Twenty-Seven

Soon did the queen return and lead me to still another chamber. No doubt a guest room, it was beautifully appointed with a high, canopied bed and a soft carpet underfoot, already warmed by a fire in the hearth.

Queen Rowena ushered me in and said, "I suggest you rest. 'Tis what you need most, I do not doubt. Beside the bed there is a bell you must ring if you need aught. A maid, named Jessie, will come."

I peered around the chamber, but softly lit at the moment, and caught a glint from across the room. A large, free-standing mirror stood there, winking at me like a malevolent eye.

Lady Margaret's eye, perhaps.

In panic, I cried, "I am sorry, but I cannot stay here."

"Why ever not?" demanded the queen.

"There is a mirror!"

Once more, I covered my face with my hands.

"Goodness!" Swiftly, the queen summoned her servants. "Tak' the mirror awa'," she ordered quietly. "Are there any others in here?"

"Only the hand mirror, your highness," answered one of the maids, with a curious stare at me.

"Best tak' that also."

When they'd gone, Queen Rowena touched me

lightly on the shoulder. "What a fuss! But there, the mirrors have been removed. Get some rest, lass. Would you wish a meal sent up?"

I shook my head, wanting only to be alone.

Soon, I had that wish. Avoiding the windows for fear I might see myself reflected there, I took shelter in the bed, which was reached by three steps.

Exhaustion swiftly found me. For a time, I remained senseless in the deep quiet. Thereafter, though, I heard voices—either a dream or an overheard conversation, I do not know which. Close at hand, they sounded like Kenzie's voice and the king's.

"I would no' lie to ye, Father. I never have, and am not about to begin now."

"You maun admit, son, the tale you ha' told me is your wildest yet, and difficult to swallow. A witch and a tower, and a rope made of plaited hair—"

"That is your grandchild she carries."

"Can ye prove it? Others may ha' scaled the wall o' that tower in your absence. And from her point o' view, you are a ripe plum to pluck."

"Am I?" Kenzie sounded angry. "The youngest son of a king who has a string o' sons, and blind to boot. Aye, such a prize!"

"Still, who is she? Does she possess a surname?"

"Not any I know."

"Well, then."

"You may no' believe in her honor, Father, but can ye no' believe in me? If I tell ye 'tis truth, will ye no' accept it for my sake?"

King Maximillian made a sound of disgust. "I would do most anything for your sake, lad. And young men will sow their wild seeds. But for you to say you wish to wed wi' her—"

"I will wed wi' her," Kenzie declared.

"Despite everything?" the king asked sternly.

"Because of everything. I believe there is a reason why Anastacia rejected me. 'Twas a miraculous occurrence that will allow me to wed the woman I love."

"Love," the king snorted. "Her?"

And even in my sleep, my cheeks burned with humiliation. Having seen me, King Maximillian could not imagine how Kenzie might love such a woeful wretch.

"You love Mother," Kenzie whispered. "You maun know what it is, to pledge the heart."

"My love for your mother has grown through many years and many shared experiences. I fear, lad, what you feel goes by quite another name. It may be lust or, seeing the lass, enchantment."

"I thank ye," Kenzie said bitterly, "for your faith in me."

I heard the door of the chamber open and close, and realized they must have been standing just outside the room. Now I heard Kenzie grope his way across the floor and stumble up the steps. He joined me in the bed, where he wrapped me in his arms. No dream, this, I thought. But a nightmare? Oh, yes, indeed.

****

My fate had never rested in my own hands. From the moment I'd been born, the ability to choose had been taken from me. When I had, against all odds, tried to exercise my will by rejecting Jeremiah Cole, I'd been punished severely with the gradual loss of everything, including my freedom.

Waking up in that luxurious room the next morning, safe in Kenzie's arms, I realized it had not been so unequal a trade as I'd feared. For though I might have lost my world piece by piece, much had been bestowed upon me.

For Kenzie was my all. I needed no more than him.

I lay and watched him sleep, the dear face I loved so well. The broad, once-smooth brow now bore tiny scars left by the thorns through which he'd battled for my sake. A tiny frown came and went there, as if he entertained troubling dreams, and his thick, brown hair lay in a tangle. His eyelids—now closed—also bore white scars, deep ones, as did his hand, flung over our child protectively.

His family might not believe I loved him, but I did—I did. And it came to me as I lay there in the clear morning light, if loved him, I would have to give him up.

Voluntarily, for his sake.

This time at least, the sacrifice would be of my choosing.

****

"My family will come round, RapAnn," Kenzie told me earnestly. He paced the floor in front of the bench where I sat. Already, unfamiliar with the room, he'd tripped over the edge of the hearth and almost knocked over a small table. "They may fuss and fret, but they always relent in the end."

"This is not one of your exploits," I told him as calmly as I could manage. "This is about accepting me into their family, me and this child I carry. It's about believing it is your child."

"I ken." Distractedly, he forced his fingers through

his hair. "Why is that so difficult for them?"

"Because it matters so very much." Because they could see me, as he could not, and had trouble understanding how he might tie himself to such a wretched creature.

Kenzie sank down onto the bench beside me and took my hands. "They will accept you, once we are wed."

"They will not."

"I will go at once and mak' arrangements for the ceremony. Something quiet, I am thinking. There is a small chapel here on the castle grounds. Would ye be happy wi' that, RapAnn, or would ye prefer a grand celebration?"

"I do not want a grand celebration, or—"

"Just the two o' us, then? Aye, perhaps best, given you carry our child." He caressed my belly gently.

I drew breath that fluttered in my throat and set my pulse racing before I said, "Kenzie—I fear I cannot marry you."

He froze where he sat, my hands still in his, and his expression went as blank as I'd ever seen it. Always, always Kenzie shone with life. Even in our quiet moments back in the tower, where he'd shared my confinement, his energy, both of body and mind, had been palpable. But now he stilled, like a man stabbed to the heart.

"But—" he protested. "But you must."

I wondered how he meant that. Why must I? Because of the child? Because, in rescuing me, he had assumed responsibility for my welfare?

Because he loved me?

Because he had decided so, just as, all my life,

others had made my decisions?

Similar thoughts must have raced through Kenzie's mind. He paled, his tan face going almost gray. "RapAnn—I always intended to look after ye. Had it no' been for Anastacia and my father's promise to her father, I would ha' proposed to ye at the outset. Now life has given us that chance."

I said with calm I certainly did not feel, "Yet many things have changed."

God help me, I did not pause to think how that might sound to him. I said what I said—and broke my own heart—for his sake. He deserved better than me. But I forgot he'd already been spurned by another because of his blindness. And he could not see the tears in my eyes.

He shot to his feet. "Ah, I believe I understand you at last. I misconstrued your feelings, did I? Indeed, who wants a blinded husband?"

He blundered away across the chamber, bumping into furniture in his haste to leave me.

His name formed on my lips. "Kenzie—" But I refused to speak it.

Far better, for his sake, that he should go. Better he think me selfish and ungrateful for all he'd suffered on my behalf. The pain of that, or so I believed, would be far easier for him to bear than that of being tied to me for a lifetime.

Chapter Twenty-Eight

So you see, those who tell my tale always miss the truth at the heart of it. They speak of a beauty locked in a tower, yes, and the evil witch who kept her there. They tell of a blinded prince but they never explain what happened after the spell crumbled and the maiden's world along with it.

In those tales, it's all about the hair. Perhaps that's correct, after all—for my hair represented my beauty, and of that I now stood shorn.

The days that followed my parting with Kenzie were among the most difficult I'd ever endured, and that is saying much. I missed his company. Its absence became a physical ache that seemed to affect the child, for it kicked within me wildly. I longed to see him, to explain what I had and had not meant by my words. To tell him how I loved him.

But the break had been made. He was better off without me. After all he'd sacrificed, I could make this sacrifice, in turn.

I felt as if I'd crawled out of a hole into the sunlight, only to jump back in and pull the dirt over my head once more. Almost better, I thought, if Lady Margaret got word of my escape and came to reclaim me, return me to the tower or put me in some other prison.

Lady Margaret did not come, though I had plenty

of other visitors. My maid, Jessie, cared for my ordinary needs as once Elsie had, and saw me every day. A physician and a midwife both came, examined and advised me. I received visits from several of Kenzie's sisters as well as the queen.

Kenzie did not come to my door.

I told myself I was glad of it, all the while his sisters chattered about him, and hinted how unhappy he was. I insisted I was relieved. My little maid—far kinder than Elsie had ever been—fussed over me and said how prettily my short hair curled around my face, and I could not help but wonder how it would feel if Kenzie ran his fingers through it. I bitterly assured myself it was for the best, while the queen inquired about my plans for the future, making me believe she wanted shed of me.

While our child grew.

Then, one day, the queen again came to me, sat down upon the settle in my chamber, and folded her hands.

"Mistress RapAnn, the king and Prince Kenzie ha' come to a decision. You are to be moved to the quarters that were originally prepared for you, a cottage outside the castle walls."

A cottage? Aye, back at the tower, Kenzie had mentioned one. But why now? Did they wish to distance themselves from me? Perhaps they could not bear to look at my ruined countenance. I did not know, but any sentence preceded by *the king* must be obeyed.

"Yes, Queen Rowena."

The queen, not an unkind woman, looked upon me gently. "I am sure ye will agree, 'tis for the best. You may ha' your privacy there and will receive all you need to live."

A charity case, dependent once again.

"Of course," she added implacably, "we will need access to the child."

Fear spiked inside me. Would they take the child when it was born, even as I'd been taken from my parents? Only if they believed it was truly Kenzie's.

I might lie. Say someone else had climbed up into the tower. I might, if it assured me I could keep my child. But for the life of me, I could not make myself do so. Those moments Kenzie and I had clung together in warmth and belonging—the only real belonging I'd ever known—remained far too precious to me. I treasured them, treasured *him*, too much.

So I said nothing, merely bowed my head.

I moved to the cottage two days later. Strangely, it turned out to be very similar in appearance to the tiny house where my parents lived. Hard up against the curtain wall of the castle, it nestled in a small scrap of garden.

Where grew a bed of rape.

I saw it on my way in, while amid an entourage that included the queen and several of Kenzie's sisters, along with a train of servants.

The child kicked inside me, and a wild craving arose within. I wanted that rape, as I'd rarely wanted anything.

The cottage, though small, offered all I could ask. The main room, heavily beamed and stone-walled, had a tiny kitchen on one end. Attached was a bedroom. Comfortably furnished, the place boasted mullioned windows, all with window boxes that overflowed with flowers.

No mirrors, not a one.

I had few possessions of my own, no need to unpack. Kenzie's sisters fluttered around the place and left with the servants. The queen remained.

"RapAnn, I hope you will be happy here."

"I will be comfortable." Happiness, as I knew, tended to prove elusive.

"Should ye want for anything more than we ha' provided, just ask."

I wanted Kenzie, with bone-deep longing, but I didn't say so. I merely nodded.

After she left, I went out and gathered some rape leaves. I ate them thereafter, every day, until my child was born.

****

Not all stories have happy endings, even though we might want them to. When we sit by the fire of an evening and someone spins a tale, when we hear of the hero's great trials, we wish for the satisfaction of knowing things have worked out as they should.

But truth is truth, and I'm here to tell you, things seldom do work out fairly, or right.

If they did, I'd never have been taken from my parents. I wouldn't have been raised in a world of illusion, where magic spun the reality. I wouldn't have been shut away from the world for most of my life.

I will admit, I lost touch with reality in those last days, before my child was born. I had troubling dreams wherein I found myself surrounded by mirrors and heard Lady Margaret's laughter. She'd had the ultimate victory, for not only had she ruined my life and destroyed my appearance, she'd made sure to blight my future.

My child arrived on a beautiful, late spring morning, and with relative ease. I'd heard stories of great travail, but for me, it was not so.

For months, I'd been certain the child would be a girl, another such as myself to suffer imprisonment. But he arrived a lusty boy with a crop of thick brown hair and so much life spilling from him he could not be mistaken as any but Kenzie's son.

Everyone came to view him—the queen first and then, at her second visit, the king. All Kenzie's brothers and sisters arrived. Even Kenzie's great friend, Justin, who viewed the child somberly before giving me a long, thoughtful stare.

The queen said, "He looks so much like Kenzie, when he was born."

I kept silent on the subject. I lived in fear that they should decide he was theirs after all, and, believing me unworthy of raising him, take him away from me.

"What shall you name him?" the king asked. He gave me a level look. It still bothered me when people gazed full into my face in that manner. "He will need a proper name."

What was proper? I did not know, so the child remained unnamed.

And Kenzie did not come.

I no longer craved rape salad. But as the days spun out into the warmth of summer, I sat often in the garden with my child.

And I sang to him.

I sang all the old songs, the ones the birds had taught me back in the tower, the ones I'd made up to ease my loneliness, and those burned into my heart. I sang to my small son because I wanted him to know beauty, and he waved his tiny fists, and smiled and smiled at me. It made me laugh the way I used to laugh with his father. No one else.

The castle grounds—even those outside the walls, abounded with folk on any given day. It came to be that when they passed my cottage, they hushed their voices in order to hear my singing.

And one day as I sat in the warm sunshine with my son on my knees, a shadow fell over us.

I looked up, and my song faltered in my throat.

"Please, do not stop singing," Kenzie said. "'Tis so beautiful."

Tears flooded my eyes. Hearing his voice—just seeing him once again—destroyed my composure, for which I'd fought so hard.

"I heard you singing," he told me. "Please, may I come in and listen?"

Chapter Twenty-Nine

The heart is a curious instrument—tenacious and difficult to discourage. You can beat it down, wound and batter it, but it will rise up again at the merest glimmer of hope, like new leaves in the spring.

Like the birds that always, always returned.

As a bird, Kenzie made a right handsome one. He wore a bright blue half-cape over his customary hunting clothes, a pair of dusty boots, and a tentative expression. His scars had faded, or perhaps the bright sun that bathed us there in the garden merely washed them from view.

He asked, "Is he there wi' you? My son?"

"Yes."

"Aye, I should ha' known. 'Tis to him you sing."

I sang to both of them, but I could not tell Kenzie that.

"May I—see?" Not the word he wanted, to be sure, but neither of us possessed a better one. I nodded and cleared my throat.

"Yes, of course."

He came down the garden path and past the patch of rape, moving in that new way he had, as if sensing the very air. I slid over on the bench and reached a hand to guide him down.

"Here."

We sat, so close our knees touched. I guided his

hand—beloved hand—and placed it on the child's head. "See?"

A smile broke across his face when he touched his son's cheek. The child kicked his feet and gurgled, and we both laughed.

"What shall you name him?" Kenzie asked. "It should be something regal, with weight to it—Gregory, perhaps."

"It is a goodly name."

"Everyone says he looks like me."

"Oh, he does. Strong—you can feel how strong he is. With brown hair and, already, a look of you about the jaw. He has your eyes—" I faltered.

"I hope not. My eyes ha' failed me. They cost me the one thing I valued in this world."

"Nay, Kenzie, nay. It is I who failed you. I am the reason you lost your sight."

"If you believe so, RapAnn, then why send me away because of it?"

"I did not. I did not!" I began to weep, and the child commenced crying.

"Whisht," Kenzie bade me—or both of us. "Then why did ye reject me?"

"For your sake. Because I, your family, and all the kingdom know you deserve better than a nameless wretch with a withered countenance."

"Is that what this is all about? How you look?"

"I have lost everything—even my hair, my one remaining beauty."

"But ah, lass, ye should know how I see ye in my mind! The fairest flower that ever sprang up in any garden, though ye were forced to grow in a dank prison."

"That is not the truth."

"For me, it is, RapAnn." He once more grasped my hand. "What if 'tis you who canna' see the truth?"

Through my tears, I asked, "But I did. I gazed into the mirror and saw what had become of me."

"RapAnn, list to me. Not one person who has met you since your release describes you as aught but lovely. From my father, to my sisters and brothers, all ha' confirmed your beauty."

"Impossible! I saw—"

"Justin has suggested magic."

"Magic?"

"Aye, Lady Margaret's malevolent brand. My love, what if she enchanted not your face but that mirror into which you gazed? Just another o' her cruelties."

Another of her cruelties.

"RapAnn, my love, what if you never changed?"

Slowly, he drew an object from the pocket of his jacket and extended it to me. A very small mirror it was, oval and with a filigreed border, probably gotten from one of his sisters. It sat on his broad, brown palm winking at me, like an eye that held all truth.

"Oh!" I cried.

"Look, RapAnn," he urged. "Look into the mirror and remove all your sorrow."

I could do that. I could, for better or worse, gaze upon what the mirror fed me as truth. There was truth, indeed, and then there was belief. I sat there with our child on my knee, bathed in warm sunlight, and waged an inner battle, perhaps the fiercest one of all.

Then I leaned forward and gazed, instead, into Kenzie's wide, sightless eyes. There in the clear light of the garden, they reflected everything back at me—the stones of the cottage at my back, the bright roses spilling around the door, a patch of green rape.

My own face.

I laid the mirror aside carefully. I wished to incur no more bad luck. But I needed no mirror, for I could see the truth in the eyes of my love.

And that love gave me all—all I would ever need.

A word about the author...

Multi-award-winning author Laura Strickland delights in time traveling to the past and searching out settings for her books, be they Historical Romance, Steampunk, or something in between.

Her first Scottish Historical hero, *Devil Black*, battled his way onto the publishing scene in 2013, and the author never looked back. Nor has she tapped the limits of her imagination. Venturing beyond Historical and Contemporary Romance, she created a new world with her ground-breaking Buffalo Steampunk Adventure series set in her native city in Western New York.

Married and the parent of one grown daughter, Laura has also been privileged to mother a number of very special rescue dogs and is intensely interested in animal welfare. These days while she's writing, you can always find her latest rescue, Lacy, nearby.

Her love of dogs and her lifelong interest in Celtic history, magic, and music are all reflected in her writing. Laura's mantra is Lore, Legend, Love, and she wouldn't have it any other way.

Thank you for purchasing
this publication of The Wild Rose Press, Inc.

For questions or more information
contact us at
info@thewildrosepress.com.

The Wild Rose Press, Inc.
www.thewildrosepress.com